GW01367286

THE SWIMMING POOL

THE SWIMMING POOL

A Novel by

Ralph McNeill

ARTHUR H. STOCKWELL LTD
Torrs Park, Ilfracombe, Devon, EX34 8BA
Established 1898
www.ahstockwell.co.uk

© Ralph McNeill, 2016
First published in Great Britain, 2016
All rights reserved.
No part of this publication may be reproduced
or transmitted in any form or by any means,
electronic or mechanical, including photocopy,
recording, or any information storage and
retrieval system, without permission
in writing from the copyright holder.

British Library Cataloguing-in-Publication Data.
A catalogue record for this book is available
from the British Library.

ISBN 978-0-7223-4596-2
Printed in Great Britain by
Arthur H. Stockwell Ltd
Torrs Park   Ilfracombe
Devon EX34 8BA

CHAPTER ONE

'You've got a long life ahead of you still . . . but I see you have already crost the bar . . .' said the fortune teller, frowning, scratching the side of her face with long, crudely coloured fingernails.

'Already crost . . .?' Robert Dawson looked up. What was she talking about? He could hardly have a long life ahead of him and be dead at the same time, could he?

He glanced about the small room but the charmless, discoloured, damp wallpaper told him nothing. The crone, head bent, continued to study his palm, both her small mollusc-like hands holding either side of his, as if scrutinising a spineless book. Wasn't bar an archaic word, and a poetic one at that? Crost being the obsolete form of crossed. Of course, there wasn't any real reason why the old girl shouldn't read poetry in her spare time, and be influenced by the picturesque terminology, though, he thought, shied clear of recognisable culture in case it corrupted or perverted her natural gift. Only ten or fifteen minutes earlier he had climbed the stairs up from the street to the crone's room, having passed by below on numerous occasions on his regular way to the library. He had promised himself to pay her a visit, attracted by the sign creaking on high, old and tavern-like, depicting a strange, variously designated hand, a network of cracks superimposing and contrasting or contradicting the original painted divination lines, though seemingly in no danger of threatening the solidity of the sign itself. Finally, a sudden whim had given concrete reality to what should have remained in the class of mused-upon unlikelihoods. An inexplicable strengthening of a feeling that should have dissipated itself by the time he had impulsively gotten around to it.

'Very odd, very . . .' said the old woman. 'I haven't seen such a . . . such a . . . before. But there it is.' She let drop his hand without warning and it fell with a clunk on the table, a piece of malfunctioning human technology. She stared at him with narrowed eyes. 'You been to anyone else?' she asked, as if he could be holding back on a competitive interpretation.

'No,' Robert answered truthfully. Or what he took for truthfulness, given the absence of any considerable memory. For where could any morality get its resonance from if not an unobscured past? 'I thought I would try you first.'

And that was the truth. Except that it might conceivably give the impression that afterwards he'd be going elsewhere for a second opinion, which he had no intention of doing. By definition, the uncharacteristic was a one-off. And naturally (memory or not, Robert believed that his previous prejudices had been condensed into another set of reliable instincts) he didn't believe in this kind of thing, though dimly realised that what he assumed to be his kind of sceptical mentality was the sort that got the best out of it, not being prepared to sacrifice what had been intuitively apprehended with a temperamental dismissal of the lot later on, when the mood wore off. Not that he was overtly excitable these days, if ever he had been. Periodic indigestion could suggest a now mostly spent volatility of spirit. A spirit so intrinsically connected with his memory and pathetically lifeless without it. But the mysterious bar business still remained unresolved and he started to wonder if the fortune teller wanted something over and above her stated fee to elucidate on it. Though coming up the stairs (authentically unswept, the carpet made threadbare by countless feet) he'd had the definite feeling that he was not about to confront a conscious trickster. He'd had the unmistakable impression that she would be in possession of a genuine power, an unfeigned talent.

'Have you ever died on the table?' She looked directly in his eye, devoid of any other-worldly affectation.

'What?'

No, he hoped it had never been that bad, though he wouldn't have been surprised had he passed out in an armchair or two, even slept the night in a flower bed. For he sensed an unremembered journey from full forgetfulness to the room he now occupied. Initially disturbed, he'd gone to see a doctor, tried to explain his peculiar amnesia, but had been treated unsympathetically, a work-shy malingerer after a sick note, eye on the main chance of an incapacity benefit. But like so much he was unable to substantiate, it was all true. There were no years growing soft like toadstools that his sore, spontaneous thoughts could rest their heads against. When he looked for understanding to the past, to the years gone by, all he saw was the vague, unintelligible graffiti of a theology of time he could make no sense of, couldn't appreciate for its decorative style alone. Yet he retained knowledge of objective, abstract manipulations, practical usage, only personal experience stripped away. This hadn't meant though that he felt like a newborn, all vulnerable quivering flesh, no; behind his eyes a screen of understanding like crushed history made all the difference, showed him where the booby traps were, how you could never learn from experience but strangely kept doing so, how many meanings danced on the edge of a smile, the epic communications compressed in small talk. . . . Then the two weeks' memory to be getting on with, memories prosaic enough to belong to anyone and possibly indispensable for it. Hard memories no amount of constant digging could change, romanticise.

'Surgical operation,' the fortune teller elaborated irritably.

'Twenty-two minutes over on the other side.' Her eyes blinked rapidly as if she mentally flicked through a book of records. 'Looking down and seeing your physical self stretched out on the operating table. . . .' She was obviously an aficionado of the more speculative television documentary.

Robert Dawson sat back in his chair, his palm still outstretched, a stubborn supplicant. This was a thought that hadn't occurred to him before. That he had been involved in a serious accident, had been near death, when rushed to hospital, doctors and nurses running presidentially on both sides of the trolley taking him to the operating theatre. He had practically died. Instruments registering heart activity had failed, and regaining a peculiar kind of consciousness he'd had an out-of-body experience, his spiritual self floating about the ceiling, attracted by a powerful, irresistible light, a potent nimbus, a great force of unknown energy. From the balcony of the undead he had felt blissfully safe, all enigmas illuminated, not wanting to come back, ecstatically returning to his real home after so long away. . . . And then it all snapped. What felt like a thread snapped and once more he was back into his earthly body, partially conscious, indecipherable voices drifting in and out of his head, memories rendered useless, broken at the spinal cord of recollection, vague shapes trying to create a world, one he could relate to, because that ethereal feeling was wearing off, the anaesthetic reclaiming the victim, leaving him cold, numb, and alone. . . . Only it hadn't happened like that, not quite like that, for such an experience would have left a scar, an articulate cicatrise, a series of voluble if healed wounds. . . . He shook his head with the knowledge of his unbroken skin.

The fortune teller tutted, annoyed at Robert's difficult palm. It wasn't any distinctive uniqueness that baffled her, but rather the teasing ambiguities there.

Roughly she took up his hand again. No one's idea of a seer, a diviner, her ordinary dress took on a rare, esoteric significance, the department-store bandana masking her forehead seemed to be emblazoned with cryptic symbols. This, Robert supposed, was the modern unaffected way of her kind, no longer keen to stand out and be condemned in the mall as a 'traveller'. She would be on good terms with those in the corner shop, gossiping, backbiting, discussing last night's reality programme, the fatalistic tendrils of the storyline of a much loved soap opera. Anything alluding directly to the occult would be avoided at all costs. Except when she was taken aside for a private whisper, an appointment made. Only her closest friends knew what she did for a living ('a wonderful knack she had, you know') while for the rest she was vaguely eccentric, colourful, uninterested in sexual matters. Old friends knew what went on in her dingy office up three flights of squeaky steps, though she acted the kind-hearted, soft-headed clairvoyant, her comprehensive knowledge, her profound inner life unknown to them, if guessed at occasionally. So in this she was able to live a double life, one to which she was perfectly suited, for most who opened their palms to her revealed themselves as dichotomous personalities.

'Illnesses?' the fortune teller asked, interrogatively.

Well, if he wasn't responsible for his problematical palm who was? Yet the point of intersection was so – so –

'Tumours? That kind of thing.'

So many of her clients left it for so long. Not that things would have turned out other if they'd dropped in before, but . . . Eye contact at this stage could be awkward because the middle distance was wafer-thin and two-way between them. Yet he took her uncertainty as further proof that she wouldn't make some sensational if formulaic fiction just to catch his wallet, that in the end her desire to be just another old – elderly woman out on the modern streets would be granted, that she would be the nobody or unexceptional person of her dreams. And yet he sensed her to be a very genuine talent, put to pathetic shame, destroyed, by creeping, ineradicable, ubiquitous urbanisation. Though he too was a lover of the streets and their centreless mazes. To have surrendered his hand to another for so long gave it a feeling of unusual heaviness, as if empty air supported all this time took on the consistency of a cannonball. As if his fate really did have an unwieldy density. But he couldn't understand why she was having so much trouble with the surface impressions, making out a case for unfathomable obscurity. He would have snatched his hand back and read it off himself but was afraid of appearing rude, impolite. Suddenly he grimaced painfully as with visible frustration she dug her sharp fingernails into his soft (and here was a relevant sociological discovery) flesh. But he did sympathise with the old girl's predicament and was absurdly pleased not to be gifted so himself. As far as he was aware. This being the automatic refrain attached to all his thoughts nowadays.

'No – no, not that I can recall . . .' he answered, embarrassed.

How was he to keep explaining all this prelapsarian absence of information about himself? Although some sort of lengthy convalescence could account for his present condition. A gradual period of recovery from some malady or another, the slow journey out of some obscure affliction to a more desirable state of health. Subject to such a regime his memory could well have been jettisoned along with the complaint, could have been the complaint itself. The mind's infected chronicles had to be destroyed if he was to survive into a sane if homeless future. After his successful recuperation things became less defined, difficult to describe, but he would have found his way to his present accommodation, had been in possession of the practical faculty that enabled him to negotiate with the Department of Social Security along with other unrevoked knacks. How to open a fridge door, how to switch on a television set, how to ride a bicycle, how . . . and of course his name. Apparently losing your name belonged to another species of amnesia. His name had been stitched on to the collar of his ravaged psyche, an intangible garment that had stayed with him. It made him feel a little better to think that he had spent an indefinite period getting over an unknown ordeal, mending in a villa surrounded by beautiful, consoling countryside, rather than locked away in some hellish ward, hatching his escape, running across a grey, desolate landscape, chased by guards or supervisors armed with long-needled syringes spilling with knockout drops.

'Oh well, I'm sorry but I can't help you,' the fortune teller told him, letting go of his hand again without warning so that it fell against the bare tabletop with that dull clunk, quite lifeless, till attacked by twitches and spasms and Robert hid it in his lap, shielding it with his other hand, like a wounded creature.

He looked up at the fortune teller with undisguised disappointment in his eyes. But she didn't really seem too distressed herself, as if failure made her feel closer to that ungifted ordinariness she tried to promote among her friends. If she gave up paying rent on the office perhaps she could apply for a council flat, qualify for housing benefit, even a disability living allowance. He saw her in her room in the evening watching television, wondering why she'd been beset with such an unreliable endowment. Under the old woman's perfectly frank expression Robert got to his feet, nursing the unread hand in the other, concentrating on it, using all his willpower to coerce the paralysed hand into some kind of movement, eventually getting the fingers to waggle comically, the thumb to jerk up and down like a mechanical lever. So in retention of its secret it had conspired in its own resurrection. After this he plunged the hand into his jacket pocket and after scuttling among the small change there brought the hand out and invited the fortune teller to take those coins that constituted her fee.

CHAPTER TWO

After the devastating fire the library had been rebuilt exactly as it was before, brick by brick, window by window, book by book. Even the piece of abstract sculpture that had stood outside and was blackened out of all recognition by the rampant flames had been cleaned up and now stood as before, gleaming in the sunlight. And the majority of borrowers agreed that this was the best thing to do. There had been talk of building a new, modernistic library, a glassy, high-flying teahouse, but sensibly this had been dumped. Robert heard about the fire (that had broken out during the night so there were no charred borrowers to bury) only after he was safely ensconced in its resurrected twin. But he too approved of the literal reconstruction, feeling comfortable in the new place as he certainly would in the old, felt its walls to provide the sanctuary he sought, that his trembling limbs were grateful for. He admired the polite, well-spoken staff, these custodians of the best of imaginative thinking and intellectual speculation. So he had felt at home, seemed to have a natural rapport with books, picking and opening to read many a paragraph at random and having a potent feeling that he had read them before, experienced the unforgettable texture of the language. So what was he to make of all this? And of course there was more, much more. There were the respectable, unemployed familiars who stared at him and quickly averted their gaze when he looked back. Very different from the others whose sturdy, intransigent expressions made them strangers for life.

He did not recognise everyone who came in, who sidled past the counter staff, eyed a vacant chair which instantly became theirs. Many had faces distorted by unknown passions or frozen desires never to be guessed at. He imagined that his own must be like that to a certain extent. It was those he somehow recognised but could find no other background for, no other lost geographical reality for, that disturbed, puzzled him. As his short-term memory grew (deceptively by leaps and bounds because so much emphasis was given to mundane detail, supposedly mundane detail) others moseyed in, some as replacements for those who had disappeared and of course had left no detectable forwarding whereabouts (had left the library like unreturnable books, furtive borrowers who had been sucked into the gritty eddies twisting about the outer doors). At first they looked bewildered, a little scared, until daily routine dulled such obscure fears, and then they assumed bland expressions, heads buried in books as if they wanted nothing more than permanent distraction. Sensed and sought the curious oblivion to be found behind words. Though after a short while they felt themselves to be in a safe place, would glance about in an attempt to assess those with whom they shared the library. Eventually their emboldened eyes would find Robert, who usually refused to engage in eye contact, thought that it was a silly game. Yet he hated being under any kind of surveillance, and thought that of idle curiosity to be the most obnoxious of all. Under persistent, moronic eyes, he would move from chair to chair in a kind of contemptuous flight, but the idiot eyes followed him, searched him out, and became questioning, defensive, imploring, accusatory...

'Robert? Are you there? I'm going to my room. But don't forget your promise.'

Robert, hands gripping the back of a hard chair and straining to loosen blocked, constipated memory, called out, 'Wait.'

He knew that the woman outside was Luis Mitre, and yet, he did remember their arrangement. How could he not? An amnesiac never forgot anything the second time around. And they were practically living together nowadays. Only a remote, undefined sense that this wouldn't be the best for them, at least in Robert's mind, prevented it so far. He had managed to communicate this to her, delicately enough, without putting her off for good. With a short-term memory, no matter how progressively and consistently developing, he placed considerable importance on his senses, on the inarticulate wisdom of what seemed revived and resurfaced faculties. Luis was about five years younger than Robert, though had features that could change the nature of their youthfulness at any time. She lived in double rooms on the ground floor (Robert had the attic room reached by a sudden emaciated twist of stairs) and was generally a temporary – Robert called it erratic – typist. They had met casually on the stairs and he had chatted her up, surprising himself, discovering a disturbing philandering instinct, a lady-killing flair previously unsuspected. During a first date he had disclosed his absence of any substantial memory, and Luis, with a display of minimal astonishment, had put this down to a lack of proper exercise, had quickly set about drawing up a list of relevant callisthenics, which she assured him would release the blocked-up, costive memories. Robert thought that she was a natural improviser, that like a child she thought that consummation, fulfilment, was embedded in the idea.

'In you come,' Robert said, opening the door. 'Don't stand on ceremony.' Luis slipped by him as if the door was on a strong spring. 'I was about to have a coffee. Care for a mug before we go?'

Luis had a very contemporary face and would have enjoyed amnesia herself, would, unlike Robert, not be overly concerned about a lost past. So for her Robert was a very modern man, even a postmodern one, and so quite a catch, she thought. She looked at the chair that Robert had been valiantly wrestling with only a minute ago and after convincing herself of its reliability, sat down on it, crossing her legs, wriggling about to get composed. Exchanging facetious banalities (humour like certain abstract utilities seemed carried over incognito from another time, place, age), Robert spooned coffee from a jar into two mugs and triggered sweeteners to mix with it. Of the two refreshing processes he'd had to think twice about tea-making, while to do coffee was practically automatic. He didn't bother to tell her about his visit to the fortune teller because now it seemed a rather pathetic, superstitious act on his part, something he was unable to justify. Also he hadn't told Luis about the peculiarly familiar faces at the library. He knew already that she would think that such threatening familiarity existed only in his mind, that in proper daylight all his qualms and doubts and anxieties would dissolve into nothingness.

'Did you buy your trunks?' Luis asked as she took her mug of steaming coffee and pulled a face.

They were going swimming that afternoon. Off to the pool. As part of her infallible system to re-motorise Robert's stalled memory swimming was inescapable, even better than jogging, even better than rope-climbing, than handstands. Sex was at the top of the list although this was usually indulged in at the end of the other, less erotically climactic exercises. Professionally she had warned him not to think in terms of a . . . universal panacea. For to have your lost, mysteriously constricted memory restored wouldn't necessarily solve all your problems. In fact this could well be the beginning of a whole raft of others. Like a bodyguard his memory could have taken a bullet for him, was lost or cerebrally wounded because it had done its age-old duty. . . . The idea wasn't that crazy; the mind wearing memory as a bulletproof vest. He laughed, attracting Luis's attention, and she got him back on track. He had no knowledge of swimming though shadowily grasped the subject. It appeared his recollections left behind a patina of their individual-link contents, spectral images, ghostly reflections. He could hear the shouts, splashes, the thwacking of diving boards – see the hawklike figure of the lifeguard walking the edge. Though really, Robert was only doing it for Luis's sake. All this exercise was getting him nowhere. Except that he might look a little more toned up at the library in the morning. Only a few days ago doing the rope-climbing bit over by the bridge he had lost his grip (that frayed rope could feel like piranha teeth in his hands) and almost broke his back. Luis had giggled before clapping a hand over her mouth, rushing over to make sure that he wasn't paralysed for life. No, it was a crazy, inexplicable idea, but Luis was like that. She was on a different level from other people.

'What do you think?' Robert took the new swimming trunks from a drawer and handed them to Luis, who held them at arm's length and considered them with an expert's eye.

When she had first said that swimming was next on her list of exercises (she had given out the contents of her singular inventory one by one) for the retrieval of his memory, he had sensibly tried to argue her out of it, but being a woman of assertive nature and determined faith in her obscure remedies for whatever her friends were currently ailing from (she'd had a craze for attempting to cure her friends' various infirmities since childhood days, though it had never occurred to her to train to become a conventional physician) she would hear nothing of it. She said that the atmosphere alone was enough to cure, heal, his forgetfulness, his peculiar amnesia. She meant the enclosed sea-like ambience of the swimming pool. Robert had given up his opposition in mid-gesticulation or agitated sentence and bowed his head in submission. He realised with pleasure that she was genuinely trying to help him and cared about his welfare. She had spontaneously devised this hopefully therapeutic method in a truly selfless sense, to give him something to believe in, which was odd now because as he could open a fridge door, operate a cooker, knew which side of a bus stop to stand, and not to embark on a conversation with the voice in a lift, he was beginning to think that a memory was obsolete anyway, any memory. Wasn't it just so much cumbersome baggage? Most men waking up in a small, comfortable room and given a signing-on day to look forward to each week would think they had gotten away with murder.

'Very nice,' Luis finally allowed. 'Although the small, jolly crocodiles back and front don't seem to be in keeping with the spirit of the thing.' She shook the trunks as if the toothy reptiles might fall off and scuttle away across the floor like happy cockroaches. 'No ducks in at the time?' she added.

'Why ducks?'

This was the moment when Robert Dawson discovered that sometime in the past he had been treated satirically possibly as a child, and hadn't liked it. Though someone in a time unknown to him had been in the habit of speaking to him in a patronising manner. If this person had been a brother or a sister, a parent or even an employer he couldn't, of course, say. This person certainly could have been a periodically nasty mother or father, even a wife, and this too was the first time that he saw a wife out there (or the concept had occurred to him with a formidable intimacy), a wife whose face could only be of confusion and anger. Perhaps sadness. The frustration of not being able to recall greatly multiplied his choice, so that he seemed attacked on all sides, overwhelmed by untold malign characters. Glowered at by a composite and enormously powerful antagonist. For a moment he lost his balance; he staggered and ended up face down on the bed. Groaning, he turned over and stared blankly at the ceiling. Frowning, Luis came over and asked him had he been drinking? Robert made a definitive silent O with his mouth and then audibly said that he had only suffered a little giddy spell. Devoid of a memory there was more room in his head for incongruous material to rotate in. Luis smiled and handed him his trunks, as if he could derive strength from them. On his feet he recalled Luis's remark and re-examined the silly pattern, the tiers of inanely grinning crocodiles, and was on the verge of re-experiencing the presence of his supercilious adversary somewhere in the room.

'I'll turn them inside out', Robert said, 'if you think the crocs will threaten the virility of other swimmers. I know how vulnerable people feel in the water.'

This of course was a jocular supposition because the bathtub on the second floor was the farthest out he could remember being.

Water, he thought, was the antithesis of memory. Anyway, he laughed, nervously, exaggeratedly at his own joke, and added another more risqué jest about the trunks falling down in the shallow end. Luis's blank or suddenly vacated expression seemed to indicate that she was deciding whether or not to laugh herself, carefully weighing up the degree of bad taste it contained (any subconscious criticism of her exercise regime) and if any of it was excusable or not. Like many self-declaring unconventional females Luis had set very strict standards for herself. All her going against the accepted values was really a demolition procedure for recycling the basic materials of orthodox morality and common sense. If a lot of her behaviour was zany this was as a direct rebuttal of the indefensible absurdity of life, the world around her. She hadn't said as much, but Robert could occasionally see how her mind worked. For himself, he seemed at times ghostly, haunted, unreal, fragmentarily delineated. Was memory really the adhesive of authentic being? Sometimes at the library he felt he had literally disappeared, become infinitely permeated, myriad rays of light piercing him like golden wires. Or he was just that moment materialising there, an insubstantial figure on a chair, holding a book of lies. That too was his perception of those others, the strangers and the familiars, who suddenly seemed conscious of being there, as their heads jerked upwards as if from ultimately ineffectual sleeping draughts.

'I hope you'll like my swimsuit,' Luis said, demurely, head a little slanted, 'but you shouldn't see it until we're there.'

Luis had a good figure and possessed real female modesty, not just a version of male reticence. She also had genuine womanly humility, little sleepy moments of un-self, which made her flashes of self-assertion all the more intriguing for Robert. Occasionally, funnily, he felt bashful before her. Not having any recollection of previous sexual encounters this affair with Luis often felt like the first to him, as though before he'd been a virgin, his first orgasm with her a complete, unprecedented surprise. But instinctively he knew this wasn't so. 'My hormones have erotic memories that other parts of me have given up for dead,' he thought. Rolling the comic trunks up in a towel he thought without prurience of the kind of swimsuit Luis had under her outdoor clothes. He visualised it as the sort of costume worn by athletes, very functional and for some unknown reason very arousing. Robert who had already glimpsed bikini-clad women reclining in sunny gardens or absurdly clipping hedges had fought with himself not to laugh. He much preferred the businesslike gymnastic swimsuit. This excited him, the idea of her body gripped so tight, increased his love and affection for her, that she went to all this trouble for a man she hardly knew more than he knew himself. But wasn't that the nature of love? A couple whose increasing knowledge of each other never lost that first innocence, that intimate, possessive strangeness. Yielding to his passionate embrace he held her in his arms, feeling the smooth sensuous hardness under her flimsy dress, effortlessly transferred to his own hidden skin, that he experienced as an integral part of his own identity, like a taught skin of memories soon to be revealed.

CHAPTER THREE

It was the end of summer and the exhausted heat lay heavily over the field. Robert viewed his domain with pleasure and pride. He liked to think of the field as his domain while realising that every other boy along the back row with access to a veranda thought of the field as his private property too. But that didn't devalue or curtail his sense of individual ownership. Though on another level the field wasn't anyone's property, not even the council's, not even that nebulous authority the Crown. In a certain light that could occur at any time of the day it could be clearly seen that the field belonged only to itself. Standing up on his toes, as if borrowing a little from next year's increased height, he strained his eyes beyond the farthest perimeter, the slaughterhouse. But a curtain of blasted heat rose up and he saw nothing but obscure concealed shapes. That didn't matter much because he wasn't intending to go beyond the ditch, at its reed-trapped deepest, along the front of the wire fence that encircled the slaughterhouse. What Robert wanted to do was get some good drawings of the variety of reeds there, and in particular the noble and longevitudious bulrush. He wanted to put them in the painting he was currently working on, have them in the forefront of the picture, so that he could exploit detail, even attempt what one of his art books called a trompe l'œil (French, literally 'deceives the eye'). At least he would attempt this exciting illusion for the lower border of the painting. He was beginning to appreciate texture too much to play this trick all over, even if he had the patience and skill. But the idea amused him and could be effective in controlled areas. Robert liked to see vividly in his head what he planned to do, see it as in a waking dream. He liked to think that somewhere his paintings existed in a finished state before he started to mix his paints.

So with drawing pad under one arm and coloured pencils in a slim tin in his jacket pocket he carefully descended the steep veranda stairs leading to the backyard. It was still very hot, but like his father he always wore a jacket, for all the extra pocket space was indispensable. Still, the top button of his shirt was open, which his mother thought a uniquely summery concession. Yet it was the summer holidays and Robert felt that he had a certain personal liberty and his tie remained with the others hanging alone in his wardrobe. He stood for a while on the cracked path that his mother called demented rather than crazy, pleased that her neighbours failed to understand her superior sense of humour. The cracked paving stones led to a dilapidated chicken run, a quite terrible business, that had been left to slowly disintegrate after his granddad had passed away. His father would have nothing to do with it. All chicken runs in other backyards were in perfect order or aspired towards perfect order, were freshly painted twice a year, but Robert's father would have nothing to do with chickens, said it was cruel, 'bestial', to wring their necks, or chop their heads off like a barbarian, or mix specially prepared pellets with their meal and watch them choke horribly to death behind the wire. And although Robert could see the artistic paradox of the chicken run in such a state of dereliction, the ugly transformed into aesthetic beauty, he did occasionally wish that his father was the sort of man who could take out a box of tools and fix the run up. He could imagine helping his old man paint it. He could imagine listening to the conversation of the chickens at night. The chickens would know nothing about death and the impending chopper and their talk would be about the greatly improved accommodation.

Squeezing through a space in the wobbly palings Robert was out on the edge of the field and immediately sensed that indefinable quality of freedom. This wasn't new to him, was indeed one of the unfailing delights of the field, its scent gathered from all the wild flowers. He thought that he loved the field more than any other place, even though his experience of the world was very slight. The Seven Wonders spoken about at school bored him, and although progress couldn't be stopped that bored him too. He fixed his sight on the corrugated line of the distant slaughterhouse and went towards it, choosing one of the grass-flattened pathways he thought the most direct, though all could be frustratingly wary, perverse, practically circular. They did in fact all overlap, intersect, and were all diversely one. But you had to make many choices and believe that they all went separate ways before you found that out. Robert never asked a friend along with him when out on a drawing expedition because they soon started to complain (though they had agreed to come along with alacrity) and tramp back in the direction of the almost imperceptible row of houses, which looked like a legion of stationary ants in the distance. So he went alone, like a hunter after his game, alert to all possibilities presented to the keen eye. One day he would put all there was to put into one huge canvas, not leaving out a single detail, every point in the universe seen through one indivisible point, and then throw away his brushes.

Happening across a cluster of buttercups he regretted not bringing along his watercolours. Still, he couldn't pass these up. He would do a quick sketch with his pencils and make some subtle colour notes. His mother would like them when he worked up a proper study. She liked simple things, but often ruined this by striving to be complicated, intellectual. He thought his affection towards her was at its height though could never equal the exorbitant love for her as a child. His father had always been distant, august, awesome, except at Christmas when he became strangely sentimental, using the kind of soppy words his stern face would deny a few days later. They were beginning to take him seriously now as an artist, not just their little boy with a knack for drawing. His art teacher with his measured praise in school reports had helped here, plus the two imaginative paintings accepted for the exhibition at the town hall. Yet his dream to go to art school one day was still in the realm of the inconceivable, the practically unheard of. The more plausible fate of the grim, insatiable factories of Silvertown awaited mythical Leaving Day. That the times were supposed to be a-changing seemed nothing but a fashionable notion to his parents and one not to be trusted. Only the great sun-absorbing hulks straddling the highest rim of the landscape had any reality so why waste your time dreaming? Yet his father had once taken a test himself and got on in life.

Finishing off the notated sketch of the buttercups (including a monster of a yellow-striped bee relentlessly zigzagging about and more obsessed with the drawing than the actual flowers) he moved on, un-stung but speedily, determined not to lose sight of his reeds, the proud, helmeted bulrush. Developing his interest in art had lost Robert a few friends, some from undisguised jealousy, others from a declared but suspect inclination to regard his kind of boy as effeminate, not destined for geezerhood. But he was more annoyed with those who had alienated him just as his talent had become more generally appreciated and he was beginning to look like someone who actually might escape the Venus-flytrap streets. On good days Robert told himself that he would be happy to work in a shop or office. Though really he knew that such a graceful resignation was due to such a time being in the unimaginable future. He knew that one day years would be only as big as a sugar cube but now they were the sizes of boxes you could climb into and still have room enough for your train set. Only a few of his mates (his mother went virtually apoplectic when he used that word: 'Chums, darling, chums') stayed with him, weren't threatened by his art, had projects going for themselves. And he had been told discreetly by his art master that he shouldn't be too surprised if shortly one or two girls stepped into the vacancies left by his disloyal comrades.

Sometimes at night he could hear drifting through the open window of his bedroom the pathetic cries of animals as they went down with a thud in the slaughterhouse, as if such stifled anguish stored up during the day was sharper received then (mixed with a thin coating of pornographic film over his inner eyelids). The slaughterhouse staff though were engaged with a special order, piling carcases into panting trucks. No one in the streets remarked on this any more (Robert imagined a golden age of profound vehement protestation), turned silent heads when guns sounded during the day. He had once painted a cow facing his aproned executioner and callow apprentice as a surreal or primitive family portrait. The focal point was a skilful pained look of brave ineluctable mortality in the cow's eyes, one that it was supposed to be too clever or too daft to comprehend. This painting had won the silver ribbon in an inter-borough competition and had been reproduced in the local newspaper. His father hadn't been impressed, or feigned not to understand the picture, and gave him a pound for a trip to the Tate Gallery to educate his naive vision. How his father even knew about the existence of the famous gallery was never revealed. Nevertheless, Robert was amazed. He had been overwhelmed, inundated by another world of formidable scenes, styles, exotic apparitions. A kaleidoscope of dazzling colour, and marvellously applied greys, earth pigments. Later, Robert had sat in the tea room in an unbreakable trance. For him the world had changed and would never be the same again. For a whole week he'd been completely destitute, experiencing the utter loneliness of not being able to draw or paint. Wearily, he had started to wonder if it had been some dreadful machination on his father's part. How could he possibly compete with anything in that many-halled building of breathtaking masterpieces? His mother regarded him as if he had been initiated into disillusioned manhood by a day's pass at a bordello (the word she would have found for the nearest council flat of ill repute). But he recovered. As the great visions receded his own pictures intensified with a new vitality, a new verve. He returned in a state of fatigued forgetfulness to the world he knew best, those familiar scenes that in the painting of them revealed that he had his own vision to nurture.

Side-stepping a brigade of stinging nettles he got his first whiff of the ditch (at a time when food smells as such were unacknowledged) though it remained out of sight. A few allotment sheds stood about, broken, damaged, tomb-robbed by vandals, or showed the blond patches of new planks conscientiously carpentered by pea-

stringers now at work. No other boy or man was to be seen, and far from feeling lonely he experienced a wonderful intimacy with all about him and with the invisible company he always sensed at such a time. Being alone and simply observing had become for him such a natural state that he was hardly aware of it. Hence to the secret pleasure of his teachers and parents he had become a mature, detached boy. Perhaps too detached. For under such an intense gaze the pointlessness of what others did was often made painfully apparent to him. Robert of course made no judgements, rather marked the composition, the way the different parts worked together in harmony. Some aware of this innocent inspection of all about him felt the little they did increased, given extra meaning. Though he had his terrible lapses. Much of importance slipped away unseen. No one knew what he lost, what was sucked away forever into the black holes of innumerable blind spots.

Previous summers had seen Gypsies parked in some parts of the field – his mother disliked him using that word: 'Romanies, Robert, *Romanies*' – but this year they hadn't appeared. He hadn't really noticed this until now, and for a fraction of a second he hallucinated his favourite caravan of past encampments, the brilliantly decorated fortune teller's caravan. He actually saw it beautifully poised between two rickety allotment sheds, its amazing colours heightened in the sun. But there was no grazing horse and no florally dressed fortune teller. Then in a blink of an eye it was gone, like a giant butterfly, its enormous fragility expired, leaving behind a dreamy emptiness. Robert was struck imagining both pictures merging into one and producing a very weird and wonderful creation. This he stored away for a future painting. He had seen many voluminous gowns in the Tate Gallery and knew he could do one himself. He thought of painting the horse and meticulously depicting each hair of its fly-swiping tail. The problems involved in drawing and getting exactly right the positions of the wheels, the wild, primitive, uneducated brats ('Children, please, Robert, Romany young ones') and the beaten, cowed dog, eyes infinitely dejected and hateful. It was the kind of picture he could work on all through the winter to keep him warm.

The ditch was very wide and once rumoured to have been a proper river. Certainly Robert didn't dispute this and watched its mongrel waters with respect. But generally the ditch was admired for being what it was in itself. For being muddy and for supporting a variety of plant life. Though only very small and timid and uninteresting fish lived there. After rain the green murky surface looked very beautiful, almost translucent. When Robert came close to its edge he sat down, consciously wearied now by his journey across the field. And now his head seemed to swim, to reel. He pushed his art materials away from him as he always did when feeling unwell, unaccountably ill, depressed. This was the power for good or for evil that he invested in his art. His eyes though remained fixed on a clump of tall bulrushes he'd spotted at first and which he intended to draw, get down in part as potential candidates for his picture in progress. But now the advancing weariness gradually erased all artistic aspirations. (This was his first intimation that he would never desire anything as he would desire sleep.) He laid down his head on his drawing pad like a flat, un-plumped pillow. As he did so he heard voices shouting, unintelligible voices, and from one eye struggling against the powerful allurement of sleep he saw the green murky surface of the ditch lift up like a tide, rise up like a great un-repellable wave – formidable, threatening, sun-occluding – and then crash down on him. As he went under gasping for breath, arms flailing wildly he saw an obscure shiny face coming towards him, a face distorted by the agitated waters, and then felt his wrists gripped by hands, strong, determined, human hands.

CHAPTER FOUR

They went to the local indoor swimming pool and when Luis came out of her cubicle on the other side – the ladies' and gents' changing rooms faced each other across the sparkling water, strangely archaic but agreeable – Robert thought that she looked... Well, he was lost for words. He couldn't recall seeing a woman in a swimsuit before, but he didn't find the concept unusual, just visually unfamiliar, a little strange. Though he felt that he would have been struck in some kind of way by the first sight of Luis in her costume no matter what. The tight clinging body-colour suit with its border of pale flowers seemed to him more sexy than actual nudity. This applied to the others as well. It had something to do, he surmised, with the way the women moved along the edge of the pool, as if ordinarily dressed, when in fact the verdict of the eye was that they were only a blink off from utter nakedness. Undressed in the bedroom a woman could be more natural, creaturely, and so oddly enough (after the initial erotic surge) less sexy. Too available to be truly desirable. What you went on was memory. Now though, Luis had surrendered herself to Robert's appraisal, and even with other attractive females prowling about could be in little doubt as to his inner response. Robert, jocosely, made a thumbs-up sign (signs, gestures, like abstract knowledge seemed carried through the memory gap) and Luis smiled, turned, and dived in. The water opened up to receive her like a chalice.

It was then, watching this practically miraculous bodily

performance, that Robert was to have the experience that was to change the life he didn't know he was living. He felt that swimming was a complex business and it was only the frequency and the commitment of the swimmer that made it look effortless. Like love, the previous spadework disappeared in the first kiss. But it seemed that Luis thought swimming as natural as breathing because she hadn't bothered to instruct Robert verbally or even like a mother guide him in other ways. She had left him to his own obscure devices. So he felt terribly stranded on the side and cold fear sliced through his heart. This filled him with shame and he immediately resolved to do his best. He took a deep breath, looked for a clearing, and jumped in. His body seemed to enter the water in precise instalments, numbered parts, conforming to the labelled areas on an anatomy chart. Then as his back cradled under and his head was dragged along with it he had a vision. Light burst around him, like a silently exploding nimbus, or luminous depth charge. It happened so quick and was over as quickly that when he came up, all in a prolonged instant, there was nothing left to it, no light, no hazy, nascent memory. Just a few unrecognisable images like moth wings over a flame. Swimming horse-like to the stairs he started to feel tired, his neck pained him, his limbs ached, his feet felt withered and useless, as if he'd done several lengths of the pool or had been swimming frantically out at sea. When he got out, slithered on to the side, he found Luis sitting there, peeling off her cap with a look of concern in her eyes. After a little while he sat next to her, legs dangling in the water. For a minute or two they sat in silence listening to the strange tennis-court echoes of joyous swimmers, the aqueous tuts of water broken by divers. The violent arm-slamming by the irrepressibly obstreperous. About the pool's edge, hands clasped behind his back, like a young god contemplating the sport of the mortals below, walked the lifeguard.

'Well?' Luis said eloquently.

There seemed to be in her eyes something of the light he'd seen under the water but less brilliant, but again nothing opened up to him in it, though he would have been shocked, unnerved, had he been able to discern images of any kind. He looked away.

'Well? Well, what?' He wasn't even going to attempt an explanation.

She knew something had happened to him but couldn't guess what, and neither could he. It was only logical to assume that he'd been given a glimpse out of his old life and that for some unknowable reason this had been snatched away, instantly erased, or returned to its incredibly small space in the universe. But he wasn't going to fall into the trap of trying to elucidate on something that no longer existed even as a perception. Even thinking like that pushed it farther away. And what reason did he have to believe that what he had perceived had any real significance for him apart from the indefinite intuition that some part of his mind retained an ambiguous promise that it had, that a deep impression had been made, some probably unreliable fugitive endorsement. Usually such convoluted cognition only plagued him at the library or during nights of insomnia when no discernible past to examine for character defects nearly sent him over its own edge. He had thought swimming would purge his excessive anxiety, but what had happened had only exacerbated the threatening obscurity he felt all about him.

'It's really you, Luis,' Robert said at last, deciding to regard her laconic 'Well?' in a less cerebral light, to bring it down to a more manageable level.

Luis smiled and self-consciously touched the strap of her swimsuit. She always looked a lot younger, almost girlish, when pleasurably abashed. His own trunks were as Luis had astutely assessed earlier, inane, moronic, gutter-pressy. Though as yet no one had laughed at them outright, perhaps because a victim suffering from amnesia has about him all the superficial abandonment of someone who can take care of himself. Now this intrigued him. Everyone likes to imagine himself a tough guy from time to time, it's a decisive way of putting an end to periodic harassment, but to what degree should he allow his mind to embrace such indiscriminate experimentation? Live and learn, he supposed, must be the motto. Watching the variegated, spontaneous activity in the pool he wondered how this could go on without common consent and general concurrence to some elaborate regulatory system similar to the codes used on the motorways designed to avoid head-on collisions and other accidents. Yet once you were in there . . . he supposed it was all a matter of coordination, and that by comparison people were more flexible, subtle instruments than cars and other relatively ponderous vehicles. He watched swimmers tunnelling and worming their way underwater, some narrowly criss-crossing, and wondered if they had dreams, recollections, visions. Was being underwater the next best thing to being asleep? Yet it was a peculiar oblivion that persisted after you had risen, come up again, keeping its secret intact. A sleep that left you more tired than before.

'Thinking so much won't help you,' Luis said now, as if unaffected by his compliment.

Though the shouting about her was often like constant accolades, easy loud unforced praise. But she was annoyed with him. She turned her face away. Did he call that swimming? One jump off the side and he seemed to think he was finished, had completed a full afternoon's exercise. While she (the originator of the system) had gone from one end of the pool to the other in a strong, vigorous overarm and didn't think she had started yet. Still, she couldn't really blame him, and he looked so pale and shocked. . . . Perhaps struggling to recall if he had any swimming experience before, trying to recall when last he'd really got so wet, other than in the rain, the bath, the shower. And that wasn't the same, was it? Getting parts of yourself wet at a time wasn't swimming. Moving through water, being wholly submerged in a pool, was very different from just passively receiving it. Hygienic immersion wasn't on her list of exercises. She looked inquisitively at Robert again and was startled, disturbed by his profound degree of preoccupation, distraction. He also looked extremely sad, long-faced. This was very worrying because she had thought her regime of exercises would bring him out of himself and in that way make room for his blocked-up memories to flow again (he couldn't remember because he had left himself no space to remember) not drive him deeper into himself, where only a curious and enfeebling blankness seemed to be. She realised that she herself wasn't a great psychologist, that on paper her strategy might sound ridiculous, naïve, unintentionally humorous. Nevertheless she thought there was something to it. Luis was beginning to have considerable confidence in her essentially spontaneous eccentric ideas.

'What happens to you when you swim underwater?' Robert suddenly asked, although he had been debating with himself the judiciousness of asking such a question. 'Or don't you ever go under?'

He hadn't actually recalled the dream or vision he'd had during that brief immersion, but a certain feeling of it seemed alive in him (like a dream had at night and forgotten in the morning, an indecipherable advertisement survived for it). Or was he beginning to feel in some way encapsulated by it? That it was growing a hard but fragile covering about him? A glow seemed to surround him and he felt mysteriously protected from the outside world. He hardly seemed to comprehend the outside world at all. Sometimes at the library, observing through the window workers going back and forth, he was at a loss to see what motivated them. But of course it was memory. But now he felt insulated, detached, from the commotion of the pool. And he didn't think this was because his preciously accumulated recent memories had dissolved, been scraped off by something in the water. He simply felt at ease with everything, inhabiting a desireless state. He wanted to tell Luis about it, but of course there were no words. Perhaps above all else he felt the ineffectuality of language to explain anything. Then all the noise, the ever-berating cacophony of the pool ceased, collected itself harmoniously into one pounding regular beat, a strangely peaceful consoling rhythmic contraction and dilation. He could never (at the moment and the moment was all that existed) describe this to Luis, and wasn't afraid as the physical environment changed in keeping with the unfathomable pulse, tempo. Although feeling individually privileged it was impossible to believe himself to be the only one caught up in this exuberant oscillation, though glancing about all else did seem excluded, not aware of what he experienced. Then like time into eternity a darkness infiltrated, spread everywhere and a terrible, deafening and alien caterwauling cut into his ears. Rocking to and fro, arms folded over his chest, on the edge of the pool, he felt overwhelmed by desolation, grief.

'Are you all right?' Luis asked. He looked bad, but perhaps nothing more than a tummy upset. 'Perhaps we should go. Obviously water doesn't agree with you.'

Robert laughed hollowly. Had he been in the habit of rolling about in the mud his memory wouldn't have deserted him. Maybe cleanliness was close to godliness and amnesia was close to devilishness. But wasn't forgetfulness divine? But of course he had no idea how he had behaved prior to when his mind had suddenly stopped providing him with a discernible background to describe himself if only to himself. In a state of full recollection he could have been anyone. What he had just recalled was so blissfully expansive that it really could have included everyone, could have been universally singular in its uniqueness. A timely repetition of what he'd already seen, gone through, while momentarily submerged, it was difficult to say. But if, and this was a luminous if, Luis's regime was beginning to work, then would his memory return in parts, randomly, chaotically or chronologically, or according to a scheme yet to be revealed? Would his memory return as it had gone or would its arrangement be changed in the process of returning? In a flash he thought: 'Did I just recall my exit from the womb? Have I waved goodbye again to Eden, am now drowning in what people call reality?'

Feeling eyes focused on the back of his head he turned and saw the lifeguard looking at him from the other side of the pool. He had been talking to a couple of teenage girls laughing and thrashing about in the water, showing off, and then he had looked up and his attention had become engaged by Robert and Luis, possibly because of their stillness, the contrast they posed to the rest of the pool. There was something strange about the lifeguard, but Robert couldn't guess what exactly.

'No, let's stay,' he said. 'I'm just getting used to it. I'm just beginning to get the measure of it.'

Pale, enervated, after such a traumatic emergence, Robert slipped back into the water and met Luis face on, smiling conspiratorially, teasing. He was afraid that he would lose his nerve and scramble for the steps at the last moment. He could have no idea of what awaited him down there, what memories would be awakened. He could see from looking into Luis's eyes that she was aware of his fears, his amorphous anxieties, was partially infected by them herself, something that made her less than robust, forgetful. The recollection of a deceased memory should be a wonderful thing, to be embraced with joy, happiness, a sense of positive renewal. The return of the prodigal son with the hope of a reckless train in pursuit, only perhaps not too reckless.

Luis found it difficult to imagine what it would be like if she lost her memory (could it be like losing your heart, something she'd wished for many times?), how she would go about her life without it. The whole thing was fraught with moral difficulties. Suffering often made you a better person, a more sensitive individual, and she could tell from Robert's eyes that he had suffered greatly. It was his eyes that had first attracted her to him, the strange innocent confused light they contained. But what if a recovered memory showed him as another, altogether different, man? Someone cold, callous, selfish, egocentric . . . In fact all those negative qualities usually associated with . . . But the water was having its effect. Lapping up against her body she was beginning to forget, relax, dissociated from time. But she was used to this and did nothing to prevent it. She didn't go to the pool to remember or know about anything outside of her usual daily consciousness. If she wanted edification she could attend a series of lectures, read a good book, watch a decent documentary on the television. But she knew that as the thought of death intensified human aloneness, revived memory gives you the feeling of immortality.

Then without a word (water had its very own primordial articulation) Luis turned, performed a little elegant semicircle and commenced a slow, graceful overarm to the other end of the pool, an undeviating furrow opening up for her all the way. Impressed, less anxious, Robert decided to try and complete the same distance but underwater. As a person suddenly feeling unafraid takes on a previously inconceivable project. If anything intensely vivid and dynamic waited for him down there he now thought he would be ready for it. If he were to be exposed progressively or randomly to a forgotten past then there seemed no better place for it than below the surface where all was naturally misshapen, disfigured, exaggeratedly warped. Later on better sense would be made of it as already proved, unless of course it was all delusion, a sickness of the spirit, some intermittent unbalance of the mind. Slowly he lowered his head below the still surface and started the breaststroke. Instantly he rediscovered a rapport, a swimming skill, that he had hardly suspected of himself before. Undoubtedly he had been something of a practised swimmer, continued to hold the effortless movements in his limbs, the adept subtlety in his torso, the instinctive knowledge of how to travel through the water, not like a clumsy beginner but like someone with years of experience, easily propelling himself through the element as if made for it, air adroitly locked in his lungs. He worked his legs and arms expertly, making good progress, keeping clear of other swimmers, or flipping out of the way, fishlike. This was really good fun, and then his mind started to talk of other things.

Entering a different world, a world of forgetfulness and vivid remembrance. Silver bubbles escaping from the corner of his mouth, he saw himself (a small, younger self, but still unmistakably him) crossing a field, a field very familiar and yet threatened him with incoherent sights, as if he had something to fear from what couldn't be assimilated, digested, comprehended at once. He realised that he was a schoolboy again (both in the skin and as an invisible observer at some height) living with his parents, doing well at school, and having discovered in himself a real artistic talent. All in his life wasn't perfect, but he had no proper cause for complaint, could indeed say with only minimal self-deception that he was happy. Now he was off across the deep-grassed field (Was it really a marshland? Did he feel a certain squelchiness under his shoes?) with the objective of drawing the wild bulrushes that lived at the edge of the ditch, stood there quite rigid or swaying slightly, and were strangely evocative. Robert had developed a fascination for these particular reeds and now he planned to put their very essence in a painting, in a way that revealed their neglected beauty, their intrinsic nobility, as they guarded soldier-like the ditch. Yet so many sights of equivalent enchantment delayed him on the way, and passing an old, derelict allotment shed and seeing a silver lip of water slipping from a rusty tank his heart pummelled in his chest and he stopped for a while before going on. Under such a relentless sun distance could go by unnoticed and soon he reached the ditch, stood motionless gazing at the murky green surface alive with buzzing insects and the shipping lanes of assorted floatable junk. Tall freaky reeds like cranes lining the tussocky quayside. Remorseless heat from the sun forced him to sit down, absolutely still, staring wide-eyed at the brilliant, dancing surface of the ditch. As he sat, contemplative, selfless, vulnerable, the ditch rose up like a great wave, loomed darkly over him, threatening to fall, wash him away. . . . He jumped up and screamed, shattering the silence like a plate-glass window.

In all truth Luis wasn't a very good swimmer. She wasn't as robust as she liked to make out, even to herself. In many ways she was a woman whose enthusiasms wanted her to do things that her natural abilities wouldn't allow for. She enjoyed swimming, she loved swimming, but she was sadly mediocre. Once in the water she put on such a good show, made such a brave effort, that she was respected by other swimmers, who were probably only fair to middling themselves. Really, swimmers of any merit didn't go to the local baths. But there was a lot of competition there, if only of the skylarking, superficial kind. Almost as if to justify their near-nakedness swimmers at the pool felt under some obscure obligation to look good, even to indulge in a sort of permitted exhibitionism. Luis didn't go in for this kind of attention seeking, and would act indifferently if a male swimmer gave her a look which suggested anything other than a fleeting appreciation, had momentarily been impressed by some semi-conscious dexterity on her part. Still, vanity wasn't absent altogether and the pool was a hall of distorted and distorting mirrors. It was also a place of immense joy. She had hoped Robert would experience something of this, but she hadn't expected him to take on so much at once. She immediately saw the danger implicit of his going under so quickly (and with such a peculiar doggedness), but had expected him to surface again about halfway, chastened, which he hadn't. An experienced swimmer could easily do two lengths under, only coming up once for air at the first bar, but a full length for a beginner (and what else was she to assume for Robert but that he was a beginner?) could be very taxing. Now out of the water herself and kneeling by the side, capped head thrust forward, eyes round and searching, she saw him reforming from a shapeless blob, defining himself gradually and awkwardly and almost rolling to one side. Her heart lurched. He was obviously in trouble. Had he swallowed much water? Was he suffering from cramp? That could feel like the spearhead that had pierced Christ's side. The lifeguard wasn't far off, but was yet to be alerted to Luis's fears. Should she give him a shout, risk a false alarm, embarrassment, be accused as a time-waster? Quickly she dismissed appealing to the lifeguard and instead slid back into the pool herself, going under towards Robert, whose hand had surfaced and seemed to be blindly groping for the bar. Then his head came up, water appearing to stick to it shroud-like. He had completed his length without a break, but his face looked terribly white and his features unnaturally bloated. Luis, controlling the panic rising within, grabbed both his arms and eliciting that preternatural strength available in an emergency, pulled him upright.

CHAPTER FIVE

Robert met his wife-to-be in the last year at art school. Both had been there from the beginning of the course year, but they hadn't recognised each other and this wasn't just because a forest of easels got in their way. As there is a time for all things, so the time for love to emerge has a jealous punctuality. But she, Hilliary, was one of the group and naturally accepted as such. But Robert had never looked at her before in any romantic connection. He hadn't found her erotically alluring though he admired her bold, consciously cliché-ridden way of painting. (He was beginning to see the hidden impact of hackneyed images handled rightly.) He was getting accustomed to the idea that you didn't need to be a genius in order to do good work, that an individual slant on an existing style was a valid method of painting, of depicting an inimitable vision of the world. Though that wasn't to say that if you worked very hard, held faith with yourself, subscribed to the infinite-pains scenario, the shell of your slavish imitation wouldn't break one day and out of it would emerge original canvases, startling images, never before seen by the eye of man. Not that Robert was obsessed with greatness, with genius, in fact he had a contemptuous attitude towards it. He thought that no genius had come forward since the Renaissance. All he wanted once he had gotten over his early, studied naïvety, was to be a good reputable realist. He wasn't interested in the experimental, in the middle-class taunting avant-garde, in mixed media, though some of it seemed satirical enough to amuse him. Like him, Hilliary Dyer, the predestined love of his life, liked to see the world as it was, uninfluenced by hallucinatory drugs or the unfettered imagination, hated pretentious theorising, the rhetorical terminology of professional critics. It was something of this remorselessly unresolved archaism and an unconscious striving after an intuited lost world, that finally brought them together, revealed their perfect love.

Once they realised they were in love (it had come as something of a shock, as if their hearts had gotten together in secret, laying down emotional foundations for the future to come) they were inseparable. Such couples literally made for each other were instantly recognisable at colleges and universities and elicited great respect and envy. Other students, un-partnered, regarded them as prototypes for all future relationships, often felt an unexpressed idealism in themselves betrayed if these lovers exchanged cross words in public or showed themselves other than idealistically suited. But Hilliary rarely contradicted Robert, would diplomatically ignore his more unreasonable pronouncements or fatuous self-assertions. For as Robert discovered, as love ennobles it can also make you look absurd even in eyes predisposed to envy such closeness, such unfeigned intimacy. This degree of self-sufficiency can appear ridiculous, almost a criticism of less exalted relationships. And there are those who constantly watch you for mistakes, for doing anything less than perfect in their eyes. By less refined souls Robert's and Hilliary's un-separateness was resented, a fall often predicted. Lifted out of the corrupt world into one where shame had no existence many thought their uninhibited behaviour tactless. So gradually they were shunned, cold-shouldered. Caring only for themselves they were judged amoral, solipsistic. But like children who think they are welcome wherever they go Robert and Hilliary didn't see this, they were unaware of their own ostracism.

Some cynically disposed believed Robert cared for nothing but the perfection of his art, but he did love Hilliary sincerely, he loved her dearly. (She had a quality of sadness at the centre of her being he found irresistible.) He could see that artistically she was evolving all the time, but as he hoped this also applied to himself he was able to imagine meeting up anew periodically, cyclically, like eternal lovers. In contradistinction to his strict art he took an interest in reincarnation at this time and became convinced they had both lived and loved in former times, ages. When gazing into her eyes he glimpsed scenes from previous lives together, some no clearer than shadows, others with a kind of Shakespearian lucidity. He did little intricate drawings, but never worked them up into a full-sized painting. Once embarked on an artistic path of uncompromising realism Robert had no intention of endangering his vision with work on enticing fantasy or even glamorous metaphysical realities. Love had turned him into an obdurate pragmatist. He was unchangeably of the opinion that an undeviating adherence to the precepts of unmodified reality was what would save him, prove his lifelong salvation. All other infatuations were precisely that, false, temporary attractions. Though he had a weakness for playing the man irredeemably smitten, besotted with the fecund contrivances of Hilliary's irrational passion for him. For in the end all love was irrational, came from a place where the human psyche didn't preside. But painting came first, as he knew it did, really, for Hilliary. He would have been surprised, shocked, and disheartened, had it been otherwise.

But like a lot of people undeniably made for each other their backgrounds couldn't have been much more different. Robert's working-class background was all the fashion when he was at art school and he wasn't slow at taking advantage of this when the opportunity presented itself. Though secretly he loathed it. He hated the accent (which in his ears sounded unbelievably coarse) and he hated the cultural deprivation. He preferred to think of himself, not altogether inaccurately, as a divided, alienated individual. One who was (privileged) to suffer for others in their unconscious roboticism, in their spiritual blindness, which was peculiar considering the strict orthodoxy of his artistic vision, as it was developing, and as it was accessible to the most irreclaimably prosaic mind. Yet he wasn't stupid. He did perceive uncanny forces at work below the surface of life. While he worked hard to get the surface of a picture flat and smooth, the subject matter deceptively poised, uncontroversial, he liked to suggest hidden disquiet, some unseen anxiousness perceived obliquely. Some students agreed he achieved this, others that his paintings were dull, uneventful. He knew that he must be freer with texture, strive for a more palpable grittiness, for a more spirited rendition, without putting anything of 'himself' into what he did. But he always knew what he was attempting to communicate. Therefore it was both easier and more difficult to decide if a painting had succeeded or not. Never putting anything of himself into a painting it always spoke back to him loud and clear. For Robert realism was the supreme mystery and anything that failed to conform to immediate and unclouded perception was missing the point, being needlessly complicated and even guilty of the heinous crime of prevarication.

Hilliary, though she also thought of herself as a realist, saw no problem in including 'herself' in what she did. Rather shy, it was the only time she could. And she fitted nicely, comfortably, into a revamped cliché. Once she had taken a common perception and refashioned it in her own image she felt more alive, more paradoxically inside her real self. But she remained very reserved and never allowed herself to dominate any picture she executed. Finding herself transfigured in what other people took for granted, was what she believed art was all about. But she truly loved Robert and his impersonal vision of the world. And coming from a class one or two (or considerably higher, she confessed in private) up from her beloved her shame was of a different nature, being of that peculiar sort derived from suppressed superiority. Hence her assumed over-servile mannerisms. Her father was so well-to-do that Robert could never remember what he did exactly, but was a talented speculative businessman. But he was a nice man, a Freemason, which he freely admitted, without that aggravating clam-like concealment. (Though Robert had been careful with that first handshake, making sure air had sufficient space to breathe between their palms.) Her mother was entirely slinky. Like her daughter she was gracefully slender and when Robert first visited their home (very big, detached, surrounded by trees all in leaf, a couple of ponds) Hilliary had joined her mother on the Arabian-like carpet where they resembled much to his astonished eyes two companionable leopardesses. Mr Dyer had looked on, seated by an antique roll-top desk, drink in hand, insulated from honest toil, smiling, perfectly at ease. Robert wondered what he had done to achieve such a seemingly perfect lifestyle. Obviously a smaller version of her mother, Hilliary's sophisticated attractiveness (she wore a dress altogether different from the corduroy coat and skirt she wore at art school for the last three years non-stop and that had become her unmistakable uniform) appealed profoundly to Robert, for he had a well-developed if clandestine eye for the garb of the rich. But that evening he had left Hilliary's home cast down, having discovered a fallacious love for walking and refused a lift home in her father's undoubtedly grand car. He had never felt so low in his life though all had been done to make him feel comfortable. (Was this it? The coveted homely comfort that can supply any convenience to a virtual stranger without visible exertion?) Yet their fore-ordained love had survived this crushing experience – had been strengthened by it – and on subsequent visits he would deal with things better, wasn't so intimidated, belittled, mastered his inferiority complex, at least within those affluent walls.

By contrast Hilliary un-intrusively got on well with Robert's parents. While he stood with his back to the back door and grinned woodenly she charmed them down from their stilted embarrassment. She had no problem with those lower down the social scale, possessed the confidence and compassion of one who has no personal experience of what she willingly and lovingly embraced. Robert stood a little back from these scenes, snobbish in himself. And somewhat satirical. Assuming the stance he'd secretly hoped and dreaded that Hilliary would have taken, unable to adjust so successfully. His mother, of course, adored Hilliary, loved her manners, her unaffected joyousness.

For Hilliary was by nature a happy person, a happiness that peculiarly her love for Robert subdued, seemed almost at times to depress. And whenever he brought her home his father sat quiet on a hard chair next to a silenced radio, as if privileged to be in her presence, not shy but gratefully made inarticulate by his son's choice of girlfriend (lifelong partner, it seemed obvious), which of course reflected on himself. They also liked her paintings, her watercolours, which unlike those of Robert had real emotional power. (They sadly regretted his abandonment of his colourful animated fantasy style, his childhood visions.) For all his devotion to the art of realism, to the un-interpolated world in which they lived, Robert's paintings were often too subtle, too nuanced, for the basically simple sensibilities of his parents. Not so for Hilliary, who now explored the primitive immediacy of woodcuts and linocuts, a power lost in more-sophisticated techniques. But often they were one-shot works, Robert judged, and looked at again a certain superficiality lingered in the eye. She often discovered a fresh subject to explore before it had occurred to Robert, who because he spent so long over a painting (over art he had the selflessness and dedication of a medieval religious) was apt to be slow in recognising new potential scenes, domestic interiors, previously unobserved categories of interest.

Because of the undemonstrative intensity of their love (after a while they had regulated all amorous display) no one in the class expected them to break up and this proved a correct assumption, and by the time they left art school they were living together, sharing a flat, getting on with their own work in different rooms, but never isolated, always spiritually in communication. It was a great wrench for Robert to leave his parents and he had to endure Hilliary watching him shed uncontrollable tears when reading *Look Homeward Angel*, an extraordinary book that after having reduced him to a lump of quivering jelly he never went anywhere near for the rest of his life. He also greatly missed the view from his bedroom window, the wild, sprawling field, a different colour for each season, often under snow or flooded from the docks in winter, but how beautifully green and alive in summer, a carpet worthy of the fearful tread of cherubim, or was that the cloven feet of young devils? Later on, when married, Hilliary occasionally mocked him for his youthful sentimentality, his undisguised tearfulness, his inability or stubborn refusal to sever the psychological umbilical cord attaching him to the past. She accused him of slipping away as often as possible to see his parents, whereas in truth he seldom saw them alone, but spent the runaway time walking the old, familiar streets – the word *familiar* had a peculiar fascination for him, like a charm capable of giving form to what otherwise remained vague and indistinct, a mantra that had the magic to turn a hostile world into one of truthworthy affection – experiencing that delightful feeling of being lost among all that was perfectly known and realised.

Hilliary hadn't found an emblematic novel to help explain that period to her, or if she had kept it from Robert, revealing a private side of herself that mostly came out in company. And it was quite natural and unremarked on for her to frequently visit her parents; with or without Robert, although they liked to see him, and nowadays he didn't find Mrs Dyer so insufferably artificial. In fact he found her forthright and very natural, and was unable to see why he had once thought of her as incredibly phoney. Had that been a protective air she'd assumed till certain that her daughter was out of danger? After the first unenthusiastically accepted esoteric handshake Mr Dyer offered no more, but he generously financed their flat, though held back for the time being from buying it for them, yet to be entirely convinced of their long-term enduring relationship. He liked Robert, but secretly believed him capable of unforeseen, whimsical, regrettable actions. But he had no doubts about his daughter and would have done anything for her. Their respective parents had nothing in common and had the sense and intelligence to see this and avoid engendering false amiability. There had been a time when Robert had hoped that his mother and Mrs Dyer would discover some common ground (he had detected a streak of vulgarity in Mrs Dyer that he imagined could be with the relevant encouragement alchemised into a pedestrianism acceptable to Mrs Dawson), but this transpired to be illusory and short-lived.

At first they had few friends and really desired no extension to what they had between them. But self-sufficiency can be a vice and subconsciously realising this they later allowed others into their self-contained circle and were enriched for it, both personally and artistically. Hilliary stole a cat from a litter in a neighbour's garden (this didn't go unobserved, but was excused or ignored) and blessed the animal with an overflow of her love for Robert.

Mr Dawson died during the second year of his son's marriage and Robert had been at the hospital bedside to see his father's eyes close forever. A terrible observation only truly realised in retrospect, when in this case the sullen eyes would reopen in Robert's dreams, full of an inexplicable accusation or some desperate request. Of course when alive Robert hadn't shown his dad enough affection, enough love, had argued with him pointlessly, perversely, but wasn't this the same with all sons? Wasn't his guilt pathetically redundant?

CHAPTER SIX

'Look, friend, I'd take it as a personal favour if you stopped staring at me. Maybe you don't know you're doing it, but . . .'

Jolted out of a dream Robert looked up into the direct though unaggressive eyes of a man who only moments ago had been seated on the other side of the library, reading on one of the chairs situated between the bookshelves. These weren't the only chairs for readers and the others, quite comfortable, plushy, were arranged about a circular glass table, very modern, with conspicuous bolts attached to it. But this was a very open place and readers only sat there if they had been coming to the library for a long time, had lost all self-consciousness as to where they sat down. If by any remote chance a new reader sat there on his first day he would soon grow uncomfortably aware of his unmerited intrusion and move off, find a chair shadowed by the towering bookcases. This didn't mean, Robert had noticed, that all readers automatically gravitated towards the superior chairs around the table, for there were those who remained content to be seated on one of the unnoticeable chairs they had been initially attracted to. Robert had imagined some progressive system at first, but had abandoned this idea when he became conscious that the puzzling, obtuse familiar faces occurred in any order, that those he seemed to know from some inexplicable distant part, cropped up in any sequence, according to no analysable arrangement. In fact all the readers appeared subject to some capricious mobility which had nothing to do with securing better chairs. He himself always sat in the same chair if possible, but that was only out of laziness or a couldn't-care-less attitude. And the man who had just spoken to him had seemingly materialised out of nowhere.

'Staring? Was I? I do apologise. . . .' Robert rubbed his eyes. 'I was just staring blankly, I suppose. . . .'

The man smiled, put a reassuring hand on Robert's shoulder, and walked off, crossed the library floor and sat on a chair Robert hadn't seen him occupying before. This had instigated a bout of palpitations and Robert held his book up in front of his chest as if to conceal his distress. Luis had always emphasised the importance of breathing exercises and made them an integral part of her regime. Now they came in very useful and a feared panic attack was averted. He lowered his book and tried to find the line he'd been on before the unexpected intrusion. But life will intrude as he was beginning to discover, secret, hidden life. But this was the first time he'd been spoken to in so many words by another reader and it was a long time before he got over the violation. Sometimes a member of staff said a kind word to him if he took out a book (he had actually *joined* the library, causing another separation between him and other readers, who merely left their books on the chair when it was time for them to go) or a guard might call him 'sir' because he wasn't one of the stumbling alcoholics who occasionally did a turn of the library before being chased out. He looked cautiously at the man who had approached him to see if he was one of the familiars, but as he had his head down it was hard to tell. (Could he fit into the just-emerging category for those both familiar and unfamiliar, both stranger and unplaceable friend?) From what he had gleaned, staring, intense observation had been a profound part of his life. He shook his head wonderingly. How could he tell Luis about any of this, it was so weird, so rationally implausible. And who did he suppose he was, an amnesiac gumshoe?

Luis, who perhaps had lucid, unimpeded recall herself, believed in a rigorous drill to improve recollection, in the universally acknowledged efficacy of exercise for memory loss, or so she said. (And wasn't that how great philosophies started out? By sheer, unapologetic assertion?) And now the bizarre seemed prosaically effective. Robert was beginning to historically relive his own forgotten life. He hadn't told Luis about this, about the unexpected productiveness of her swimming exercise and now visited the pool alone. He went there virtually every afternoon (to go under and confront a kind of oblivion took courage, unusual, frightening courage), but not with Luis. In fact he had abandoned the rest of the regime. For reasons not entirely clear to himself he had stopped seeing Luis. No doubt she felt herself dumped, ditched, that he had gotten involved with someone else, and in a strictly ironical sense this was true. If she thought he was dallying about with a successor he would have to live with her disappointment, because he still held her in high esteem, had a very special affection for her. But this was one journey he had to take alone. Out there, swimming underwater, going through the inextinguishable hoop of fire, he felt his self was called upon only. If the past was unfolding chronologically as it seemed and not thrown back into his face haphazardly then regular attendance at the pool alone was the only ticket.

Light flooded through the large windows of the library like it might do in a church and illuminated the book on Robert's knee, lit up a Van Gogh painting, so that the vision looked alive, full of a wild and mystical animation. Robert, in his self-absorption, his self-surrender, felt a part of both worlds, the still library and the blazing, nocturnal landscape. Spurred on by recollection he had attempted to draw and was surprised by the degree of expertise he had achieved. Yet wary as usual he realised that the memories might not be his own. Like a dream, what the water gave him could be a guiding blend of scattered events. With so many swimmers the pool could be the home of untold vagrant and orphaned memories. There was no denying the peculiarity of the water as he went under, as it rippled velvety over his back, flowed furrily along his arms and legs, before opening the dimension of oblivion, where yesterday was variously re-experienced. What he apparently recollected could be a collation, a treasury of several lifetimes. The idea seemed fantastical (though he had considered it a lot recently) and he jumped up from his chair, catching the book as it dived towards the floor, and walked in a little frenzied circle, hand stroking a non-existent beard, before the disapproving or astonished looks of others drowned his exultancy, told him he was literally getting ahead of himself, that no brainstorm no matter how diverting should be allowed premature expression. Being himself, while at the library, a part of such a monitoring system of eyes, Robert obeyed the censure.

Recovering his previous un-agitated state he concentrated on getting back into the book (the text was unusually intelligent), finding that line (among other dancing, swimming, blurred sentences) he was on before. . . . He turned a page and picked one at random, read it through halfway and then returned to the beginning. This went on like a toy train on a small roundabout track. His few revamped memories were still at a distance, both intimate and impersonal, but thankfully not jagged fragments, which he would find confusing, probably incomprehensible. He wondered why no one had come in search of him, why he had been kidnapped so exclusively by his amnesia, why he as a physical body (and he did pinch himself while realising that a figment would have similar responses) had left no apparent discernible trace. He would have thought Hilliary at least would have tried to find out what had happened to him (he had accepted this woman as his other half though his feelings about her were equivocal at best), got on to the police, persuaded her father to hire a private detective, or instigated an investigation by herself. Or was it fated that *they* would catch up with him the moment he caught up with himself? Would a ladder be lowered down into the pit just when he had climbed up the wall and clambered over the top? He sighed audibly, attracting a number of inquiring eyes. Perhaps such efforts had been undertaken already and had met with failure. Not everyone who stumbled into the maze found their way out again.

Last time in the pool his progress hadn't gone entirely

unobserved. While he could now do the whole length underwater he could encounter trouble towards the end on occasion – though this had nothing to do with Luis's quite unnecessary interference.

Coming out of the dream, the watery death of the senses, could be a shock, induce temporary disorientation, be unhinged by a powerful sense of resurrection. There was no way of avoiding the experience of oblivion, of a trance-like sleep, while physically he continued on autopilot, like a deadly predatory fish, willed into motion while its brain was elsewhere. Waking from the dream, the recollection, garlanded with the invisible seaweed, the imperceptible algae of memory, could prove difficult, because his life was again changed. Though he thought he had mastered this, was able to break the surface with a reasonably convincing imitation of an exercise satisfactorily completed. But all remained in a state of unpredictability and on his last time out the ending hadn't gone exactly right. Why this was he couldn't say, but suddenly he had felt confused, at sixes and sevens, his legs painfully weak and his arms behaving like broken reeds, mouth gasping for air. Almost immediately the lifeguard was alerted. Walking the edge of the pool as usual, hands gripped behind his back, head bent in animal vigilance, his keen eye had spotted Robert. He took brisk strides along the edge, other swimmers swiftly, instinctively, clearing a space for the expert, the oily specialist. Outwardly not a sound could be heard and so inwardly all Robert could hear was the maniacal percussion of his own heart.

Somehow the lifeguard flipped Robert over on to his back and guided him (in a rather stately manner) to the steps. By this time Robert had regained his former balance, equilibrium, and felt rather silly, embarrassed. But the lifeguard had looked piercingly into his eyes as if he knew something, was aware of Robert's regular attendance at the pool and knew what he was up to. The lifeguard wore a skintight cap like that worn by Luis and had a strong slightly blank face, like a stone made smooth by aeons of shaping water. He was very careful with Robert as if sensing some inner disturbance. When Robert attempted to thank him the guard put a finger up to his mouth as if he was in danger of violating some code of the pool. Strength having returned to his body Robert went back to his cubicle and sat on the wooden bench, allowing himself to drip on to the floor, like a block of sculpted ice (*The Swimmer*) rather than towel himself energetically all over. He wanted time to come to terms with his new memory (for a whole family of memories orbited the principal recollection), think it over, let it settle in naturally, as if it had been there all along, needed no introduction, could soon be taken for granted. But now his inner eye was all over it, insight starved and ravenous. He usually sat in the cubicle for quite a time, arms resting on his knees, head bowed, never going back into the pool a second time, enjoying the rapturous exhaustion that now came to him as the memory sluiced his veins, numbed his mind with pure nostalgia. He wondered if the lifeguard knew that he retired to his cubicle after one swim, never went in a second time on the same afternoon, and if that was the true meaning of his penetrating look. It was a significant peculiarity and one the lifeguard might well puzzle over.

* * * * *

Feeling overwhelmed by the inescapable sight of so many books (on first entering the library each day such a sight was a liberation but soon deteriorated into a strange oppression), Robert picked up the plastic bag in which he kept his trunks rolled up in a towel and left the library and returned to his room. He wanted to think about Hilliary, whom he could see very clearly, and to see if there was anything about the memory he had missed, if there were cavities and recesses to it he had overlooked and in which other incipient or embryonic memories lingered, literal unborn offspring waiting to find life in his consciousness. (Out of earlier memories he had been able to extract better pictures of his parents, the neighbourhood in which they had all lived before the world complicated itself.) On the way in he had met Luis and although they had chatted agreeably, Robert found it difficult to conceal the fact that he was in a hurry to get to his room. On one level he would have liked to tell her what was happening to him, to carry on their relationship as before, but he was afraid of something connected with the memories, something he couldn't describe to himself, which prevented him. He was certainly alone on this one as a return to the past can only isolate you. When they parted (was she keeping up her regime of exercises alone, engaging in new and inventive workouts?) she gave him a sad smile but a bright 'See you later.' What was it about the self he had discovered in the memories that gave him care for caution? He was not altogether overwhelmed by his younger self, but few older men are. They like to think that they have made the kind of progress – intellectual, spiritual, career-wise – that leaves who they had been by the roadside looking gormless. Secretly they admire the energy-packed risk-taking though condemn what they now wisely regard as an obsessive concern with the sybaritic side of life.

* * * * *

In the evening he took himself off to a local pub for a pint. Because he didn't go in often, the welcome he received was more gratifying than had he been a much valued regular. The pub catered for those from the nearby estates. Only a few stalwarts wore cloth caps, sitting at tables playing traditional games. The type of folk that would have attracted Cezanne's eye, Robert thought. From an adjacent bar he could hear considerately regulated jukebox music, pop songs from a peculiarly bygone period, wistful and full of regret. He took his drink to a vacant table and put down the sketchbook he bought on the way home from the library the previous evening. He had been very impressed with the drawings he had been able to produce once he had allowed his hand to exercise the skill it possessed without his incredulous interference. But he had the idea that they would turn out to be nothing more than tentative adumbrations compared with the improved skill reawakened by the latest batch of memories, the artistic dexterity that was at the centre of what he now knew. Without calling attention to himself he found that he could draw quickly, accurately, capturing with precision the likenesses of those who were playing cards at the opposite table. It was almost like a superficial trick, an easily demonstrated facility lacking true psychological insight. But as he went on depth revealed itself and without too many rubbings-out, corrections, laborious second thoughts. At first his hand had seemed to work independently of his exertions, but now its manipulations felt entirely his own, his eye both guide and translator.

The attraction of cards stronger than any uncustomary distraction the regulars refused to turn their heads in Robert's direction (although there were many involuntary, suppressed jerks, and the rolling of curious eyeballs) until he got up from his chair, approached them, and humbly asked for their opinion. Still uncertain about art he thought his portraits could only be validated by those who inspired them. When he held up the pad for them to see they grinned like natives seeing photographs of themselves for the first time (did he perceive a little fear in their eyes as if secretly believing that their souls had been snatched away, imprisoned by a strange unfamiliar device or technique?), but they quickly responded with laughter and obvious pleasure, one or two standing up as if in recognition of the royalty of themselves. Robert was very gratified by their innocent, naïve response and gladly tore the sheets free and handed them out. When the landlord came over and seemed about to voice an obscure entertainments prohibition he saw the perfectly drawn and instantly recognisable faces and felt bound to relent, stood very silently, no longer willing to interrupt. Then seeing interesting facets of character in the landlord's roughly hewn face Robert got him to formally pose over by the pumps. More drinks than he might have initially cared for were bought for him and he ended up drawing faces from his own imagination, faces from recently reconditioned memories, faces circumspect, watchful, observant . . . Later, when the night air hit him full in the face he staggered, tripped and fell, landing on his back on the pavement, his deranged-sounding laughter echoing far along the street.

CHAPTER SEVEN

'Don't wait up,' Hilliary said, suppressing a chime in her voice. 'I could be late.'

'Righto,' Robert said (using half consciously an RAF cliché his father had been fond of using, had almost made it his catchphrase), not turning to see her leave the room, his attic studio. He listened to her jaunty step down the three flights of stairs and then after a few seconds' silence heard the anticipated slam of the front door. Alone. That strange sensation of being in private communion with the house. He looked at the painting in front of him and saw that there was a contour to correct. Hilliary was often late these days, evenings, and he had a good idea why. But you could hardly express your feelings nowadays even to yourself without sounding paranoid, living in a world of your own dubious devising, one thing Robert had always attempted to avoid, hence his lifelong adherence to naturalism, realism. Or at least lifelong since he had repudiated his boyhood fascination with fantasy, the colourful effusions of an overexcited imagination. But where had it gotten him, now that the art world had turned against him, turned against anything that unironically emulates photography, anything that looks like it was actually a good representation of some corner of the un-freaked-out external world. Now it was all dreamlike fancy and extreme bland experimentation. So he was out of fashion although his agent occasionally sold a canvas or two (he was too intrinsically stubborn to return to a former mode, even to one achieving success). His agent told him to keep doing his scrupulous depictions of what was familiar to everyone, and therefore what was really valued if they realised it or not. Escapism no matter how superficially ingenious was a mundane vision of life. Robert believed that his exact reproductions of common scenes brought out something missed by cursory inspection, by the usual jaded perception.

He corrected the inaccurate contour and then went on to perfect an area of dilapidated brickwork. He realised that people rushing about in the modern world had little time to stop and see with fresh eyes what that world actually consisted of, really looked like. They were immersed in a familiarity that dragged them down into a false apprehension of what surrounded them (although it could be said that this falsity, this familiarity, was essential to their progressive movement from day to day). Hilliary, finding her own kind of realism had lost ground, turned to teaching, discovering a new talent, inspiring others with her undiminished love of art. Not that she needed the income, with her family regularly boosting their (double) account. But teaching gave her an enlarged sense of self, practically changed her into another person, increasing her self-confidence. Yet there was another side to her, hungry for a kind of experience denied to her when younger, or when she thought she had no need of it, was content with a quiet, undemanding existence. But now she had developed a peculiar, passionate determination to retrieve or claim something of a life previously neglected. Perhaps in that region she was merely a late developer, but there was nothing in her expression that would have suggested this, no sudden grotesque eruptions of a delayed aspiration. But she had changed, altered under her own auspices.

Lifting his wine glass, drinking too much, he carefully added a touch to a startling delineated landscape, a study from memory. Robert had a perfect memory, no part of his life lost or forgotten, no little detail unworthy of recollection. Though how pathetic was the life he now found himself living, long gone were his art-school days, when his draughtsmanship was celebrated (at least by the reactionary masters), his deliberate rejection of postmodernism heartily approved of. Now cerebral art was enjoying its day and his hatred of intellectual conceptualisation was looked on as priggish, nothing but a right-wing affectation. That the intellect obscured true vision Robert never doubted. Like Blake he believed only the soul was capable of unblemished perception. But unlike Blake he didn't see reality as a series of contingent symbols waiting to be decoded. He believed the mystics were right, but exceeded their brief in seeing life, reality, as it really was. Robert had the metaphysician's sensibility, but without the conviction. He believed that he had lost his heaven on earth and dreamed frequently of his irrevocable paradisiacal field, now drained and turned into a sports stadium, surrounding land built on, the houses of the vulgar council type. He had charted his journey from working-class champion to defender of middle-class values and found this tragic, amusing, and inevitable. Yet it was memory he treasured above all else, as only a good bottle of red could reanimate. Each one a work of art, together a gallery of impalpable masterpieces.

Uncorking what he supposed was his final bottle of the evening, Robert refilled his glass and then turpsed out an imperfect square inch, repositioned his brush in mid-air, tipped with aquamarine.... Although it was difficult if not impossible to view your life objectively, as seen from the outside (not through another's eyes for unprejudiced vision was a fallacy) he was beginning to receive fairly plausible communications which more than suggested that his marriage was over, or reaching the point of no return, beyond which waited the chasm of viperous recriminations. Neither he nor Hilliary talked of this as just prior to the collapse of a marriage all appears deceptively charming and secure. The lull before the storm, but a lull strangely refurbished to give the impression of lasting stability. Robert though wasn't fooled (he could see all the signs as only one tirelessly dedicated to the art of verisimilitude can) and also credited his wife with distinct knowledge of the inevitable, regardless or in spite of her present effervescent manner. He knew that there were other 'factors' involved in her present uncharacteristic ebullient self, but thought that her quasi-concealed romantic attachment accounted for most, for her persistent late nights could no longer be ignored. The simple, uncomplicated happiness that comes from an unforced surrender to living in the here and now, a sainted condition that paradoxically illicit love often induces. Thought of such an unparalleled state of mind almost had him sanctioning Hilliary's unprincipled behaviour, particularly when a second bottle of wine produced a similar expansion in himself. Fairly certain that sexual consummation was yet to take place (after the ultimate pleasure has been experienced a perceptible darkness is mixed in with the joy) with her mysterious beau he did nothing for the time being (played along in his role as the duped husband, unaware of the impending crown of cuckoldry about to descend), which suited perfectly the slothfulness into which he had fallen.

Not that his work, little in demand as it was, suffered from this peculiar inertia. As long as he could remember he'd always been more productive in times of personal, emotional crisis, though he didn't consider his art as a refuge. All that he painted was a head-on confrontation with the inescapable physical world. He didn't regard himself as the enemy of fantasy or imaginative art, did in fact continue to like fair examples of it, insofar as he was allowed to appreciate the technical adroitness involved. For certain visions required an intricate architectural structure to keep their complex reveries from imploding, languishing. He realised that he hadn't made *that* much progress since leaving art school, that skill in exactitude was slow, crept along at a snail's pace, but he was willing to endure that, the pains of such imperceptible increase for future flawless work. But such perfectionism brought with it a dreadful introspection and sometimes he accused himself of being too narrow, parochial, that he hadn't travelled enough or had enough varied experience to produce a greater diversity of work. But he hadn't been interested in the exotic, or rather saw it everywhere in the common, familiar subjects he painted so well, perceiving the remarkable and strange in what others dismissed as tedious and pedestrian. It was this functional and serviceable eye (cold, as strangers saw it) that had first attracted Hilliary to him (his earlier flights of fancy his mother kept in affectionate wraps) as he was the antithesis of the archetypal flamboyant art student. Though after marriage his devotion to everyday life had made him a prisoner in his own home, a fettered gamekeeper in his own neck of the woods. Their home was a generous gift from Hilliary's father, who seemed to regard the artistic marriage as do villagers who support their local monastery in return for spiritual merit. He took a drink from his glass and held back his head, as time seemed to move differently here, in his attic, had a certain individual elasticity, as if responding to an unverifiable theorem of inebriation.

He wondered what kind of man his wife's suitor was (he used the word to himself with cynical satisfaction, though not completely annihilating his . . . opponent), another teacher from the institute or a student she'd taken an amorous shine to. That her behaviour gave her away (she was both aware of this and also thought herself absolutely safe) meant that she'd been as clever, devious, as she could in concealing the truth in all other ways, for without the game love cannot exist. The game was love's empowering circuitry. The game was Eros's meat and drink. Of course she wouldn't see it as a game because the word was too vulgar, demeaning, hardly described adequately that blissful state she found herself in. What she felt couldn't be said in anything less than classical hexameters. But a game it was and one he was expected to sit on the sidelines of, completely oblivious of the rules. There were no rules. And ruleless forbidden love greatly appealed to the heart's true anarchy. Yet the truth was that Hilliary had blossomed during marriage, she had emerged, via stages Robert had been sublimely unconscious of, from a grey and uninspiring self, a rather lacklustre personality, to someone not only undeniably attractive but who sparkled in company. (She had taken that enigmatic journey from duckling to swan – but how he loved and missed that small vulnerable creature, that shy, unassuming earlier self. . . .) Before she had not lit up in company, had hidden her lights under a bushel, but now her assured glamour was formidable to Robert, for he had taken on some of her dowdy grey feathers himself. He filled up his glass nervously, spilling ruby drops on the floor. Unaware of this gradual transformation he realised now that he had been in love with her sadness, that strange, inexplicable sadness. Now he was confronted with another woman, one no longer afraid of the shadows, a woman who knew how to manipulate her sexuality, knew she had been accepted as a little member of the society of seductresses – or at least a good screw if she had a mind for it.

Time always conducted its own revolutions when painting and occasionally he looked up from the canvas surprised at how far he had come, while the story of his life continued to unfurl in his head, almost autonomously, as if solving its own inimitable puzzles as it proceeded. Although they hadn't had any children, Robert cautiously believed that Hilliary had once had a secret abortion. Never had they touched on this (this was the first time that Robert realised that a true secret grew from the inside out, that its successive strata became impenetrable) and now if he cared at all about it, the phantom possibility of it, he didn't know how to open a civilised conversation on the subject. For the secret had fossilised to all silence. If he tried oblique words Hilliary quickly turned away and left the room. This – if indeed it had occurred and wasn't a part of his deluded, gloomy mythology – had happened several years ago when he had been on one of his deep, inaccessible, melancholic journeys, the precision over-precise, the landscapes too full of towering brick facades. Even the blackness had curious eyelets and he noticed she had put on weight, merely referred to this one evening when going to bed. Her lack of sharpness should have alerted him, but he was grateful for her disinterest, her few words of bored denial. For he was glad to get back into his own womb and suffer for the cause. Sometime later Hilliary had gone for a weekend away ('for a respite, I need a break from all this') with a friend, Molly, who had a degree in history but drove a London taxi. Alone over the weekend Robert felt the blackness lift, but watching the television which he had taken up to the attic remained his only outlet. Then Monday came around and Hilliary was back looking quite changed. Pale, suffering, staring at him from their darkened bedroom (Robert had slept the weekend nights on a sofa in the attic) with chastened, conscience-stricken eyes. He thought had he asked she would have told him there and then, though her eyes contained a touching appeal for gentleness, understanding. And what would he have said? – his faceless depression still severe and dominating. Speechless, Robert had gone away, struggled with his paints, until his own inner torment had been finally terminated. Then standing in the light streaming down from heaven again he had felt brash and irrepressible, all confidence and creativity once more.

He flung down a brush and picked up his glass. Strange how even good wine tasted like blotting paper halfway through the second bottle. He glanced across to where the old grandfather clock stood, which he had dragged up the stairs a few years ago, like a crepitating coffin. Hilliary hadn't been this late before. After class they all went to the pub, the usual intimate coterie of pubs close by to educational institutes for a tipple and chat about favourite artists, current shows. All very innocent, though many affairs originated in such groups, could be the entire purpose for joining in the first place, the subject matter purely incidental. He picked up a few clogged brushes and cleaned them with a rag, a job he liked, making sure all the right caps were screwed back on the right tubes. Obviously Hilliary's unprecedented lateness was a kind of challenge, a conscious un-ignorable violation, no excuse, bringing the previously unsayable to the surface, making the inevitable eloquent at last. But was he up to it? Every clock is the playpen of time, because every passage of time on a clock face is circular and therefore simple and childlike, while in his mind time travelled the labyrinth, was everywhere and nowhere at once. He went over to the attic window and looked out on to the night, punctuated by a scattering of stars above and the more mundane constellations of lamp posts below. The railway station wasn't far off, situated in a kind of basin, the ribbed dome higher up, discreetly illuminated, below the sleepless trains slowly wending their ways along the delusively entangled silver tracks, like a beautiful slime. He could hear the haunting but familiar sounds like an indolent jazz musician improvising from the grassy embankment, playing discordant notes for their own sake, though they seemed to Robert like obscure regrets from the engines below for having to go anywhere at all.

He returned to his painting and was immediately struck by its impersonal realism, like a prophetic if everyday window on to tomorrow. It was, he saw, a fine day. On the point of picking up his glass he heard the door downstairs shut, heard voices, muted, teasingly censored, laughter. So this was it. 'Dear Robert, meet the boyfriend. You don't object, do you? After all, there's no arguing with true love.' When it comes all the old prohibitions and hypocrisies fly out the window. Suddenly he felt like putting his fist through the painting, the picture of deceptively undisturbed life. The kind of life that would go on forever without perceptible change. In an instant he grasped the irrefutable truth of the sageful platitude that all was in a state of flux. But now he felt sunk and his anger drained away. The painting might have taken on a greater social significance with a fist hole through it, but it remained as it was before, half finished and a palpable lie to the way real life was. He had wasted his life imprisoned in a cage designed with architectural precision. He thought of the American abstract expressionists and how they dealt with the vicissitudes of life with their pots of paint and motley bicycles. But he had never really been able to let himself go and that was his tragedy. He sat limply on his stool and listened to the footsteps ascending the stairs, turning each landing up as they climbed higher till the door to the attic was pushed open and Hilliary stuck her head round.

'Oh – it's you, Robert,' she said, as if she expected to see someone else. 'This is John. He was kind enough to give me a lift. But something went wrong . . . I started to feel . . .'

They were both drunk. They should have all been drunk then, only their unembarrassed intoxication had a sobering effect on Robert. Much to his dismay everything cleared up before his eyes. On another occasion he would have thought this a terrible waste of good booze, but in the past Hilliary had often remarked that he was rarely surprised. He wasn't surprised now (in fact his feelings seemed to be throwing dice for the appropriate response), just suspended or acting absurdly gentlemanly. He hated John at once. He would have hated him if he had been waiting for a train, queuing up for a cash-point machine. John wore the kind of trendy clothes on sale in an established store fighting to get its share of the market back. Robert got off the stool and stood before the boyfriend as if he was an undisciplined class of one. For if John wasn't a schoolteacher Robert feared something drastic had gone wrong with the education system, and of course it had. He was undoubtedly a godforsaken liberal, but a man of a catholic outlook. Robert could see him holding forth in the staffroom surrounded by a clique of other unreconstructed liberals, full of high sentence. Hilliary stood smiling and apparently saying something, only the sound was switched off. Strange, it was like being underwater. That was his whole experience; he had been transposed to a different, alien element.

John put his hand out or Robert suddenly saw it there, in mid-air, peculiarly immobile. It looked both powerful enough to crush his or that like an unset plaster cast would disintegrate in the proffered handshake. Robert, unspeaking, turned away, got on with cleaning his brushes, an arcane activity to some. He had stopped caring altogether. All the dice were lined up against the wall, faces blank. He felt weary, on the edge of another desperate plunge into the intermittent nothingness he'd been foolish enough to imagine sealed over. So much of himself had been used up in punishing, unrewarding, unappreciated, ignored, oh-so-precise paintings. Now he was empty, eviscerated, gutted. Therefore a savage heroism reared up inside. There had been a time when he'd had it all, or enough that would have suited him now. In a state of such intense impotent hatred he saw his past life flash in front of his eyes. He'd had a painting in ten Royal summer shows in succession, and although the critics had been less than happy the public had returned to see them a second and third time. Also he had a small canvas accepted by the Tate (how proud his father would have been, though now it was kept out of sight in the storeroom). And prints of his work had done well in all the fine-art shops. But now his time was over, though relatively still a young man. He turned to see Hilliary, her mouth moving in, he assumed, eloquent explication, but could hardly hear a sound, only distorted noise. Grinning, tight-lipped, John, the teacher, made no attempt to explain or exonerate himself, hand gone, revoking its ambiguous friendship. Then something seared through Robert's brain and the brush he was cleaning snapped in his hands. He grimaced painfully but no sound left his lips. He staggered, righted himself, and snatching up a palette knife he lunged, stabbed blindly . . .

CHAPTER EIGHT

Just because she – Luis – and Robert were no longer going together (were they ever really going together in the sense of steadily evolving into established partners?) she was determined to keep going to the pool alone (she had always loved swimming since a child, it was where she really felt free, liberated, where she felt all her potentiality quivering with life). Certainly she wasn't going to let Robert's unexplained rejection of her move her to another pool. After all, she had found this one by herself first of all. There was something about the pool, the place, its capacity, the cheerfulness of the swimmers, the quaint fixtures, the quality of the water even, something she actually knew very little about. So once she was sure about Robert's hours there (in many ways he was something of a predictable automaton nowadays, she told herself) she could elude him, go only at those times when he was elsewhere. Probably with his new girlfriend, she thought, though he was yet to bring her back to the house, as far as she knew. She continued to work part-time (there seemed hardly any work about, her agency stammered on the verge of closing down, and she desired her freedom above all else, was, indeed, a little in love with penury) and in truth wait for Robert's aberration of mind, his strange attitude towards her, to pass. Then they could be as they were before, what they had both shared together would be retrieved, reinvigorated. She really believed that this would be the case, and then this time of desolation would be a thing of the past. Like most dropped lovers she harboured deep resentment together with an unquenchable hope for swift reconciliation. So she went swimming by herself, loved the silky water travelling over her back, caressing her body all over – gently, fondly, intimately, and yes, lovingly. For wasn't water the perfect undemanding lover, the selfless worshipper of her dreams?

But times and routines have a habit of coming unfixed or overlapping and once when Luis was in her cubicle – giving the obligatory peep above the door before stepping out – she caught sight of Robert, appearing strangely in the middle of the pool, head jutting up, mouth gasping for air. She knew it was him straightaway, like one recognises a familiar face in a crowd with only a smudge or two to go on. Obviously he was in trouble of some sort after having gotten that far from the other end underwater. The thought darted through her mind that he was performing the one exercise alone, that it had become an obsession, and the other swimming exercises that she'd had in mind for him had been ignored, or more correctly, improperly formed and never conveyed. Once Robert had started swimming underwater, she saw, he had acquired a remorseless passion. Of course, people did get attached to particular procedures, courses, and Robert must have decided early on that he was no diver, that diving had no appeal for him. Even the vastly popular overarm had little or no attraction for him. Only, it seemed, swimming underwater did it for him, whatever that was. And it didn't occur to Luis that this was the systematic restoring of his memory, reviving his lost sense of identity. Her plan or method of achieving this (spontaneous and unformulated as this may have been) had involved *all* the exercises. The return of his memory would come as a result of the successful culmination of them all. She conceived of no front man taking the overall credit.

But Robert had conceived of a passion or mania for just one, putting himself in danger, as is the usual case with solitary enthusiasms. Yet apparently he couldn't see this, blinded by an ardour that would consume him alive, or so was her fear, herself the past victim of so many uncontrollable transports. Had they still been together (and here she experienced a little flush of self-importance) she would have done her best to talk him out of it. Or attempted to modify his fervour. She would have calmly suggested that too excessive a devotion to one specific exercise was self-defeating. That he could not hope, essentially, to escape boredom. That suddenly and without any warning the satisfaction derived would level out to tasteless froth and that he would be left with nothing, exactly the state he had been in before, only perhaps more so, sorrowfully augmented. She would have attempted to break him out of his fixation and point him towards the other, equally thrilling diverse enjoyments of swimming, those he had perversely turned his back on without first trying. Plainly in this Luis would have been doing the right thing, because without a doubt his wrong-minded obsession was responsible for the difficulty she had seen him in, struggling in the water after having been forced to abandon one of his exhausting lengths. Terribly distressed, she had been about to rush out of her cubicle and dive in and save him – when the lifeguard had appeared, calm, cool, collected, having fully assessed the situation, professionally, impersonally, executing a perfect dive, the pool his unchallenged habitat. Luis had caught her breath. What a man! Then with a wholly dispassionate kindliness he had guided Robert out of his crisis. Luis's relief was considerable. But what had happened down there? Had he developed a kind of temporary paralysis? Had his muscles started to transmogrify to stone? That strange illusory petrification familiar to all athletes? She watched as he groped up the steps like a man twice his age. Had the exercise broken down and started the rapid deterioration of what he had managed to preserve since the beginning or end of his forgetfulness, leaving him practically lobotomised?

After that Luis decided not to go in and instead put on her clothes again, over her dry swimsuit, slyly leaving the pool once Robert was secure in his cubicle, locked away on the other side. She had things to do and it would have been embarrassing to cross paths, for Robert was quite capable of getting the crazy idea that she was following him about. No, for the time being she would leave him alone (or with anybody he was periodically seeing) and go on hoping for a return to normal, whatever that was. You didn't need to be with that special person long to feel the dearth of a lifetime when he was gone. Thinking that it was all wrong didn't change anything and whom had she to blame but herself? By this time, she told herself, she should be more accepting of the vicissitudes of life, only to be surprised once again that afternoon when on returning to the house she found a letter for her on the stand. She didn't open it till she was inside her rooms but had already intuited that it contained bad news. She read it over several times, but couldn't grasp more than she'd failed to understand the first time. It was from her sister Christi's husband, George, and seemed to be about an unspecified affliction Christi was suffering from. Luis couldn't decide if this lack of clarity was on her sister's instruction or simply, hopefully, a characteristic oversight on George's part. Whatever, George's eloquent reticence told Luis that something very disturbing had happened or been revealed. Luis stamped her foot in anger and frustration. She thought their rejection of modern technology nothing but snobbish affectation.

A train leaving London in the evening is always a forlorn sight and Luis felt something of the poignant sadness in her heart as she travelled towards Cromer, where Christi and George lived a quiet, even sequestered life. The note of suppressed emergency in the letter (petulantly screwed up into a ball in her handbag, its pages showed some effort of her having attempted after to straighten them out) wasn't entirely responsible for her departure, but it was certainly conducive, had awakened an irrepressible need for a change of locality, a deferment of the present pace and conditions of her life. She had slung together a single case and hoped she hadn't left anything necessary behind. She hadn't seen her sister for a long time and they weren't supposed to be on speaking terms, a conflict that continued to mean something over a distance, although Luis had forgotten the cause of this. She searched her mind and the emptiness was like a raided closet. For a moment she realised how terrible Robert's amnesia must be. Not just the closet raided, but the entire house. Was it something said between them when their mother had died? Something irreparably tactless? How a death in the family brings to the surface certain hidden truths while remorselessly concealing others. She felt the cause palpable, in its protective dark cave, but couldn't entice it through the cataract of articulation. She wondered if she would be able to incorporate this interesting image into her course of exercises as they now developed independently of any conscious scheming. Now the train rushed through the falling darkness, outside a ghostly mechanical doppelgänger kept up, full of frightened faces. Christi's husband, George, lectured on philosophy at the University of East Anglia, was a philosopher of some repute himself, a few slim volumes he'd published caused a stir. Christi, intuitive rather than academic, was self-taught and worked in a plant nursery. If only they were a little more up to date, but they owned neither telephone nor television set, their spare room packed ceiling-high with books. But George was the kind who in any age would live outside the grid, the system, regarding modern civilisation as a seven-day wonder.

Outside the train dark shapes watched them with a determined absence of curiosity which Luis felt comforting. Her sister had fallen in love with Cromer on a two-week holiday there, in love with the sea, with the red-faced crab fishermen (with the crab pots that she had thought were for cats), with the narrow fairy-tale cobbled streets, with the ever circling seagulls giving voice to the sorrows and joys of all . . . When married she had talked George into living there though he needed little convincing of the sea's inspiration, found beach walks together (the brief existence of sand castles) a profound stimulus for reflection and insight. He always took a notebook along to jot down aphorisms and epigrams as they occurred to him. Luis tried again to recall what had separated them, her sister and herself, but knew all stubborn, lasting animosities had petty ridiculous causes, that was the secret of their persistence. Now she felt obscurely guilty for having spurned Christi, had put her out of her mind for so many years, had virtually disowned her. All through childhood she had adored Christi, cleaved to her in times of gloom and dejection. Then Christi had found George at a party, revered him for his sagacity, his knowledge of ancient wisdom. Luis freely admitted that he was very clever, though she thought him too airy, an unearthly, vulnerable spirit, only partially inhabiting physical form. But he was merely reserved, often appeared like a natural hermit saved from his fate by an exceptional woman. But Luis had never been jealous. She was fairly certain that she wasn't jealous of Christi.

After changing trains at Norwich Station the remaining journey seemed to speed up and she thought that she had the strange odoriferous hallucination of being able to smell the sea long before she caught a glimpse of it through a crack in the landscape. Apprehensive, she became morbidly aware of all the different workings of the train, all the diverse and individual parts that went to make up and create the overall indivisible machine, even sensing very strongly her place in it, the inevitable journey she was on. This experience was both intoxicating and unnerving, and Luis was glad when a company employee in a white catering jacket came along, skilfully negotiating the agitated passageway between the seats, and offered her a coffee, smiling with genuine friendliness. She sipped this potent drug and soon became relaxed, pleased to have made the journey, that she had left all her cares behind. Again she attempted to recall what it was that had weakened the connection between herself and Christi, but her speculations all seemed fictitious, made up to conform to a certain notion of reality and therefore plausible, but without actually discovering the truth. She started to feel sleepy, dreamy, uninterested, wearied by the stream of shadowy shapes impressed on the window, again being drawn into the hypnotic rhythm of the racing train . . . falling, falling . . . when suddenly jolted into full consciousness, greatly relieved when they all slowed into the station, could once more stand on firm ground (for there is no land so seemingly well grounded as that abutting the sea). Politely given precise directions at the ticket office Luis found her way quickly to Bernards Road, where at the end stood her sister's house. Peculiarly translucent, real or polluted darkness seemed to belong to a different world, and she made a big show to herself of filling her lungs with fresh sea air. But lamp posts apart, all the street was dark, which struck her as a bad omen, not realising that here people lived at the backs of the houses.

'Hello, Luis,' George said, recognising her at once, long before, it seemed, she could make a positive identification of him. 'Very good of you to come so promptly.'

Luis didn't know if it was habituation to isolation (she couldn't imagine George having much to do with the neighbours) or his vocation that made him sound so formal, but she was oddly charmed by it. He invited her in and they switched on the hallway light, making her realise that before they had been illuminated only by street lighting, by the weak (deceptively powerful) lamp posts. George was of a trim build, tall, with a rich, brown voice. (Luis recalled the voice, admired its depth, resonance.) He had a full beard (not unlike those worn by the majority of crab fishermen, a few clean-shaven among their ranks seeming like boys, no matter how long they'd been going out to sea) and lively, darting eyes which could steady into deep, ironic penetration at a second's notice. Before getting his present job he had taken a poetry class at a city institute in London, the other of his twin passions, and had been held in much esteem by the students who found his understanding of obscure verse profoundly elucidating. In fact George often refused to distinguish between poetry and philosophy, regarding both as intimately connected methods of observing the same or similar universal realities. Yet in daily speech he sounded a very ordinary man, laconic and always willing to listen to what was being said. Like most men who have a voice to be liked he never gave the impression of listening to it himself. But when she'd climbed the stairs and been shown into her sister's bedroom she thought George's comparative silence could have another cause.

'Oh, Christi, you look so . . .'

On seeing her semi-conscious sister, face emaciated like a POW, Luis hadn't been able to control her surprise and grief. Was that really Christi behind that terribly withered mask? Luis moved closer to the bed though it wasn't clarity she wanted. Only immediate flight from the unacceptable was on her mind. As if sensing her distress or powerful urge to flee, George placed a captive hand on her arm. Strangely enough still with her outdoor coat on she felt more exposed to her sister's condition than otherwise. She almost envied George in his shirtsleeves, but he'd had time to get used to it, and it could only mean one thing. Perhaps because nothing needed to be said George gave her a precise account, devoid of any distracting emotionalism. Breast cancer had been detected, removed, but then the malignant growth was discovered elsewhere – digging in everywhere, entangled throughout her frail, physical frame, consuming her faster than the painkillers could work. Though there was an Alpine range of pill bottles on her sideboard and the palliatives were fighting right up to the murky yellow sightlessness in Christi's eyes. Released from George's compassionate hold, Luis went nearer to the wretched bedside, like a child brave enough at last to approach the bars on the dreaded cage.

*****

Early the following morning (Luis slept well, it must have been the sea air) after Christi had been catered for, the doctor seen and gone (a young man, taller than George with a pronounced Scottish accent), George took Luis for a walk along the beach, the sea far out, as if chased off by distantly perceived exercising dogs. After she grew less self-conscious about playing a role in some artistically photographed film she fell in naturally with George's long stride, shortened to her purpose when he could remember. Obviously Christi had been a strider too, or had become one, influenced by the sea's leaping waves. On starting out Luis had been afraid George would feel obliged to utter arcane metaphysical consolations and so was grateful for the way he only spoke when necessary or when asking simple questions about her own life. He was very interested when she took the chance and revealed her developing ideas concerning exercise, her own private methodology of callisthenics, with special regard to psychological aberrations. Luis had always been able to acquit herself well on her feet and so was particularly inspired on this beach walk. Yet something indifferently merciless about the sea always returned her thoughts to Christi's fate and she occasionally stopped as if unable to go on much farther herself.

George, no doubt getting used to a life alone, had prepared sandwiches and a flask of tea, and they sat on a sturdy upturned boat for a little break before the journey back. Because he never attempted to sing the praises of Christi it was obvious to Luis that he loved her beyond words, would continue to love her after she ceased to be, at least for him, a physical helpmate. That he phlegmatically had his agitated soul under control did not deceive her to the extent of his pain, the suffering he shared and endured. When once he used his wife's name it was like he'd stepped on a nail but had conditioned himself not to cry out. Luis wondered if he would survive his wife's death. In his self-effacing strength he was like a wounded animal who having dragged itself to the back of its cave now waits on the end or on salvation, perhaps viewing both as the same. Then, suddenly, George walked off, away from the ruined boat, off towards the wavering tidemark of the beach and faced the sea, and Luis felt deserted, terribly alone. It took her some time to realise that the howling came from him and not the wind prodded into a wild articulation. That the long-suffering man had deliberately lost all self-control, let it go, in a savage scream, a chagrined wailing of grief, no matter how selfishly conceived.

CHAPTER NINE

For a whole week Robert avoided going to the pool. Instead, he spent his days – his mornings and afternoons – at the library, like he had before he'd met Luis. But of course this wasn't the same. It couldn't be the same now that he knew about half of who he was, realised half of what had been darkly concealed from him. Actually, he had calculated that what he now knew about himself must be more than half, but that was being finicky with the remaining darkness. And he still felt split down the middle, both physically and psychologically. All his disturbingly reacquired memories on one side and all the blankness on the other. But he couldn't face going back to the pool to collect or reabsorb what was rightfully his, what in all fairness shouldn't be denied him, and yet what he feared more than anything else to have possession of. He just couldn't bear to know what was coming next, sat on the edge of his bed, hands covering his face like a frightened child at a matinee showing a horror film. Surely, he could do without the next brood of memories, the next feasibly ruinous recollection, and just carry on as he was, with the hope that what he had already recaptured would fade in time, prove flimsy and dreamlike and not stubbornly persist in his psyche and valid parts of a self he couldn't credibly reject.

In a state of contradictory attraction Robert daily felt the strange demoniac magic of the pool, the water that pulled at him from a distance, was often difficult to resist (he felt he looked too peculiar taking refuge in shop doorways when wrestling with an invisible evil spirit), but so far he hadn't yielded to its power, its ever increasing potency. Not that this inexplicable harassment stopped or started with the pool, for he had a phobia about all water in general now, had even stopped washing in the morning. He had stopped shaving, his packet of twenty disposable razors on the window sill like an unexploded pod of hammer-headed larvae. Even a dripping tap from the bathroom kept him awake all night with a nightmare he was too panic-stricken to dream. Forecasts on the radio predicting stormy weather filled him with a pungent sense of the impending apocalypse, the violent end of the world he hadn't known he was in awe of. He had only to come across water in one of its many manifestations in a library book he was reading for him to freeze, his hands to start trembling, and he was in real danger of dropping it resoundingly on to the floor, for (in his mind) the guards to come running over to see what was the matter, to slap obscure prohibitions on him before he was able to steady himself, get himself together, tell himself it was all lunacy, this fear of even the mere mention of water, and in the third person too. Yet he hadn't stopped drinking it, mixing it with his tea or coffee, taking it straight from the sink, how could he? How could he do that? But it wasn't outside the realms of possibility. Then all that awaited him was a desiccated future, an extremely dry tomorrow.

As an occasional break from the library he went to the cinema, sitting alone and if possible surrounded by unoccupied seats, staring with intense concentration at the screen. But this was the kind of intense concentration that leaves you with no idea as to what's going on, what the film is about, devoid as to any clue of a storyline, the film stars involved, what fictional characters they played, or whether it was well shot or not. All this was a blank to Robert, like what there was left of his past he was unable to recall. But at the end, when the credits rolled, his interest was alerted and he became inordinately alive to the technical side of the production, the casting, the lighting, the special effects, and of course the stuntmen. But the wardrobe and the hair stylist seemed equally important to him. But he wasn't really concerned as to who had composed the music because he hadn't heard any. Later, back on the streets, the credits continued to roll and determined his enjoyment of the film. He sat in small cafés watching the steam rise from the geyser of a hot mug of coffee, trying not to get pawed, scratched, wounded, by the serrated edge of his last, treacherous, evoked memory. Had he really killed his wife's lover? It was difficult to appreciate passion once it was over and this must be particularly true of murderous passion. Yet he was afraid to go under again, afraid to touch oblivion again for the truth that would elude him for evermore unless he could find it in him. He reflected that it was quite possible that the next connective memory in all its supposed, conceivable horror, its gruesomeness, would cancel out what had already been sorely recollected. That instead of advancing his enlightenment would push him back into the dark.

That of course could well be a desirable result. The prospect of returning to the darkness (the haunting twilight) gave him a good idea as to why it had enveloped him in the first place. How people railed against what came out of the unknown to protect them from their follies, their stupidities, their regrettable passions, the consequence of unwise actions. Now, he glanced about the library and thought it a strange thing that he had found refuge in a place that was a secular shrine to memory, the fictitious memories of uncountable characters. Yet out of nowhere came the idea that the most esteemed of these characters fought with a demon, had some weight or drag or irreconcilable contradiction on their mind or soul. Half of the fight seemed to be in appearing settled and undisturbed though few were deceived. Robert liked this place too much to get himself expelled, barred, for suspicious behaviour, particularly of the kind he would himself be unconscious of. He wasn't on the bottle yet, had no marked thirst for alcohol, though it did have an infamous reputation for inducing forgetfulness, for giving tipplers a taste of divine oblivion, and he had a perverse admiration or obscure affinity with drunken down-and-outs he saw on the streets or dumped in doorways, like human garbage sacks, their blissful abandonment of self-responsibility intrigued him. One thing he had noticed since his underwater revelations was he no longer thought that certain library users were mysteriously familiar to him. That puzzling aspect had now vanished from their faces. Some remained familiar in an ordinary way, but now there was no perplexing, unaccountable familiarity about them, and so here, at least, his ferocious staring had been erased to a more gentle or less desperate observation. Even in his present pain he watched others with less than his old, disturbing fierceness. It was as if a masking skin had been stripped away leaving them weirdly anaemic, or simply colourless in an uninteresting way. By contrast he felt himself to be healthy, sanguine, whereas before he'd been pale and bloodless-looking, almost seedy-looking. Obviously, whatever the content, memory was nourishing. There were beneficial vitamins in them. But then he touched his face, fingering his cheek nervously, and realised he had let himself go, that his salubriousness was illusory. But his fear of water was still with him. He wondered if he could rid himself of dirt with a wax compound. Didn't American Red Indians pluck out facial hair rather than use a sharp slate or the white-man's razor?

When he felt heavy-hearted, mournfully lost – although he usually felt lost in a gaggle of memories he was unable to assimilate, to properly digest – he'd occasionally have his lunch in the nearby park. He took along a cardboard box in which he had put a few edibles in the morning before leaving for the library, feeling almost the spirit of the invulnerable, dull, workman in his soul as he prepared this. Yet along with so much else, the park posed too many problems now, was far too exposed, put him at risk. The trees were just coming into leaf and were without their full heads that might have protected him from the influence of the water, for the swimming pool wasn't far off and he could easily feel the cloying sickliness of its force, the nauseating magnetism which it discharged and seemed to physically hook into his gut. It was all he could do to suppress this stomach-churning attraction. The park had the remains of a lido, very dilapidated, the surrounding wall broken, as if hit successfully by a drunken demolition ball, and yet even from its bone-dry pool, its junk scattered through, Robert felt an inexplicable power wrenching at him, making him feel unwell, afflicted by a dreadful queasiness, so that finally he had to leave the park, stumble out through the gates like a man worse for drink, or a demented fool. He could only return to his room, or to the library, where the thickness of the stone of the walls helped to deflect the enfeebling energy, make him less of a victim of an element of which he had no real knowledge – a common and universal and sublime element he now regarded as a Janus-faced god, a two-faced liquefied deity.

And what was he to make of Hilliary? Although he could now see her clearly in his memory he had no idea if he loved her as a wife should be loved. He wasn't even sure that he liked her, for the memories were both intimate and distant and in some strange way dispassionate. Perhaps his memories needed to be complete (his life *that* far, his life *so* far) before they were cogently galvanised, before they were roused forcefully into a convincing linear life scenario. As it now stood he was confronted by a terrible dilemma. And all his heart was set against returning to the pool and finding out. The pull alone was enough to make him incredibly obdurate. But he couldn't ignore or feel anything but shame because of his fear. And there was another complicating factor. On his last visit to the pool he had seen Luis there. When he had been forced to surface halfway through his swim – his emotional state on receiving the memory had reacted negatively with cramps and other severe bodily frustrations – he had seen Luis going into her cubicle, walking the edge carefully so she wouldn't get splashed. He'd had a fit of clarity and had seen her looking at him just as the cubicle door was closing behind her back. This was an unmistakable sighting and one not to be obscured by later doubts, irritating, confusing details. But their eyes hadn't met (clashed) across the pool. He knew that Luis was unaware that he had seen her, that her fleeting sighting of him hadn't allowed for any reciprocal recognition. A moment later the lifeguard was in, had lanced into the pool, other swimmers making room like threatened cork buoys.

For a while he thought that his problem could be solved by getting a job. Stop signing on as he'd been doing since moving into the room, cashing the giro somewhat shamefacedly at the local post office. Initially he had provided a false history (he had jotted down a spontaneous story of a plausible past on the back of a postcard and then compressed that into a list of jobs with accordant dates) for the DHS and up until now he had not been questioned, no one had paid him a visit. But he hadn't actually attempted to get work, hopelessly decoding the columns in the midday newspaper, doing a despairing recce of the local job centre, because he thought that to start thinking about the future a full past was absolutely necessary. Because how could you start work on an empty past? Yet even now half a past, half an identity interfered with his indigestion, gave him severe dyspepsia, acute heartburn. Given the circumstances he should have qualified for an incapacity benefit, but the complexities of applying for one finally deterred him. Even amnesia had its pride. He might well have been able to do something, though spending most of the time doubled up, suffering from a strong desire (and in the end he realised that any hankering resided in himself) to go back to the pool, go under once again, regardless of the lethal consequences. And the last revived memory had concluded at such a violent juncture, a moment of horrendous crisis (a cliffhanger that only an incorrigibly sadistic mind would contrive), he could hardly sleep at night without experiencing a nightmarish ending, forgotten as always at the crack of consciousness. Though the dishevelled bed sheets told a story for the right interpreter to untangle.

Looking at his hands (which he hadn't bothered to do, at least with any intelligent discernment since he had surrendered them to the fortune teller to read what seemed a year ago, but was probably only a week or two) it was impossible to guess what he had done to earn a living, outside of an artistic career which he found difficult to comprehend or even to hope for. During the first week in his room he had naturally assumed himself to be a worker or at best an artisan given to ideas above his station because he had no memory to police his sense of reality. But an artist? Well, he certainly had some competency. But beginning all over again as an artist was out of the question. It was all right going slowly to seed and worse in a small single room, but to lose it all while struggling to do better was pathetic. All struggle towards unrealised objectives was pathetic, much better, perversely noble, to sink forever out of sight without turning a hair. To remain calm in the face of inestimable odds was perhaps the only way to see whatever this was through. And he didn't want to be an artist fifty years ahead of his time, or delude himself that he was painting for unborn generations, canvases stacked up against the wall that would be taken out and dumped in the nearest Gahanna skip by the landlord's henchmen once he'd cashed his last giro and had gone up in an anonymous puff of smoke at the local crematorium. But the fact was he wasn't too old to retrain for some relevant work now, a computer programmer maybe, whose smiling, brainless faces he saw illustrated on most of the leaflets handed out or that were slipped through the letter box and ended up as an architecturally unstable pile on the table next to the telephone downstairs at his boarding house. In theory he had nothing against getting a box of coloured chalks and doing copies of famous works of art on pavement stones (if his untested talent was up to it), playing to the common man's and tourists' artistic appreciation. On a deeper if less lucrative level he could depict his progress in his life so far that was beginning to have a pilgrim-like aspect to it, applying the chalks hazily to the rough stone in order to achieve that spiritual quality essential to evoke nostalgia in the sightseer far from home. Though if anything he would chalk up images of the swimming pool, the shadowy interiors of the cubicles, the strong, indolent, slightly menacing lifeguard, and try to decipher the mystery it held for him, that weird, hazardous allurement of water.

The book-stacked, claustrophobic library occasionally sent him out in search of other temporary asylums and it was due to this that he discovered the cool, shady, deconsecrated churches, a breed previously gone unnoticed. Many had been turned into indoor markets, while others, still formally sacred, had their own faithful if small congregations, though not necessarily intimate. They would come and go and draw strength from their church but rarely acknowledge one another outside. Yet strangers were accepted automatically and Robert found peace there, the influence of the pool hardly reaching him there among these simple, harmless souls. Though once outside the full force of what he had taken shelter from struck him deeply, knocked him off balance, and his stomach burned with a fierce, crippling acidity. Knowing doctors were of no use to him, he bought jars of extra-strength gastric tonics, taking double the recommended dosage, but with little or no improvement. In desperation he would have given anything for an ulcer, but knew that it was the unanalysable water. It was the pustular past that was to blame, a massive boil he wanted to burst yet realised it as a disfigurement all men and women lived with and suffered from. And yet he couldn't forget that his was an entirely different case, and along with afternoon cinema, the daily accessible library, he visited the small churches in search of the historical sanctuary offered. The pain though increased, and the water, seemingly changed into a kind of luminosity, streamed through the leaded windows and over the oblivious worshippers and threatened to drown him.

Then at the end of the week he gave in. Immediately he felt two things: defeat, and the humility that comes from certain types of surrender. As if he were doing only the normal thing, no longer fighting uselessly against the inevitable, he decided to go to the pool. Strangely, at that moment he no longer felt any profound compulsion to do so. It was almost as if it could wait. He sat on the edge of the bed feeling the kind of freedom and hope that previously he had imagined could only come from a victory over the water's delirious demands. But all this quickly disappeared and it all came back and he was no longer able to resist the agonising demoralising attraction of the pool, his lust for subaqueous oblivion. His only wish was to be completely enveloped by the water for as long as he was capable of holding his breath. After his decision (and in the end it had to be called a voluntary choice on his part) he again felt himself to be a man who accountability owed a lot to. He felt that regardless of the fate that awaited him he would no longer be involved in a purposeless, unwinnable battle to avoid it. He went over to the draining board and rolled up his trunks in a dry towel, not bothering to suppress a rictus-like smile that came over his face as he gulped back a mug of coffee before setting out, youthfully skipping down the stairs with none of that pathetic elderly lack of agility he had assumed over the last tormenting week. That was all over now for he had a decisive appointment to keep. He even stopped at the crossing to think that pain, suffering, could really have a rejuvenating effect, after all.

Yes, his step was certainly springier now, now that he had given up and felt free to indulge, free to dismiss all fears. But a familiar anxiety started making its old inroads. It was not only the water, but the crucial memory awaiting him there that made him fretful, restless, though of course they were inextricably bound. Yet on his way to the pool he felt more in keeping with other people, passers-by, than he had all week. All this inner-struggling business was so alienating. Although no more than an imaginative exercise he felt a compulsion to speculate on all the possible memories waiting for him underwater, but his fictional scenarios were of a very low sort, not much above comic-book standard or uninspired screenplays. But his mind went ordinarily blank as he entered the swimming-pool building and purchased a ticket, shouts coming from inside like an enjoyable mugging. Once inside, the smell of water made him euphoric, heady with excitement, and he was glad to hide away in one of the cubicles, psyching himself up for the unknown ordeal before going out. Genuinely surprised to see him back, the lifeguard gave a mock salute, a little imperceptible bow, and with the other arm made a gesture as if granting Robert the freedom of the pool.

CHAPTER TEN

Luis stood outside her boarding house searching her bag for her key and having great difficulty with it. It was not because the key had got stuck in an awkward cranny or was buried under junk she could never bring herself to throw out or was just irretrievably lost (along with the memory of who she had entrusted the spare), but because she was fully aware she didn't want to find it. She didn't want to enter the boarding house again. She didn't want to live in her rooms. She wanted to go somewhere else, a hotel perhaps, and start life again. Cromer had changed her and so had Robert's unexplained rejection of her. So she searched her bag again and again (with a mounting exasperation that was real in the best theatrical traditions of spiralling rage) with a miraculous contrived blindness as to the key's location. She knew though, that she would need to go in again and live for a while among all that mocking familiarity before she could find another place and move out. She would need to take advantage of what she had already before she found another place more suitable to her moods, for just to go now leaving all she had accumulated (feeling as she did now, all her possessions could easily take on a dangerous air of worthless rubbish) would lead to a minor tragedy. So she relented in her self-righteous anger, and that's what it was, and in a moment unearthed her key. As she was blindly poking about with it in the lock Robert joined her on the doorstep.

A certain lucidity of the sea can make a visitor ignorant of the hardness of a life lived anywhere, but Luis had come back in a peculiar state of mind, though one she was yet to fully appreciate as seminal. For to have witnessed the death of a stranger can leave you with a feeling of mortality – after all, who cares overlong about the nameless? – but to have witnessed the death of a dear one can give you a feeling of immortality, even eternity – even or particularly in an atheistical age love is thought to last forever. On the train journey back from Cromer Luis felt herself to be in a peculiar interim, a provisional state of consciousness, vaguely suspended above herself, that both numbed her to the incontrovertible fact of her sister's death and exacerbated it, the grief she hadn't expected to feel. Christi had calmly accepted her own passing though Luis realised that her almost saintly attitude had a lot to do with the doctor's drugs. Otherwise, un-begrudged courage apart (the newly discovered bravery of the dying can be irksome), Luis thought her sister would have been wailing as her husband had done on the beach when temporarily his philosophic resignation had fallen apart, or had been deliberately relinquished so that he could feel as other, undisciplined men feel about such an intimate loss.

The sound of the key grinding in the lock made Luis think she had pulled out the wrong key from her bag and she held it up to the sky as if she had the cut of the teeth off by heart. After George had retrieved his stoicism he had been a source of fortitude for them both, as he must have been for Christi, singly, before the illness. Luis, though, had noted from the visiting doctor's demeanour that he thought George callous or insensitive to his wife's pain and suffering. And George wasn't the kind of man to make excuses for himself and to a degree expected to be a victim of the world's incomprehension. When he had first appeared on the scene Luis had assessed George as something of a phoney, but then she had thought all philosophy to be bogus, at best a nice way of feeling self-important in a university café surrounded by a doting coterie of students, but not much good when forced back into the real world, unless of course that was the trick and smartly you collared yourself a teaching post, a comfortable position, from where you could go on merrily theorising for the rest of your days. But that was before Luis started having strange ideas of her own, had embarked on her own inner journey, noticed the uninitiated casting her the occasional disrespectful glance. Had she become a phoney herself? Had she become a fugitive from natural spontaneous unaffected behaviour? And of course the first test of a phoney is to be completely unconscious of your own phoniness.

It was no fault of the key that it refused to turn in the lock, she realised, but an unresolved continuation of her own domestic frustrations. But she couldn't dismiss altogether that the silhouette of the stranger next to her on the step was vaguely unnerving. When George had broken down on the beach (as if he threw inarticulate imprecations at the sea) on the day following her arrival in Cromer, she had been astonished, and to be truthful, embarrassed. Previously she had assumed that men took pride in holding back their tears, not aware that such forbearance looked put on, unconvincing to women. Such a wild burst of grief had impressed her deeply, echoed as it seemed by the shrieking gulls. George's breakdown was very different from anything she had experienced before and she had fallen in love with him, there in that exposed windy space, without any rational prelude, fallen in love with the savage vulnerability she had sensed within the otherwise resolute, unshakeable man. George had returned as if from a normal walk, face free of any distress, bright from the chafing air. Luis kept her love to herself as, though mainly unconscious, Christi was still above the ground, although a plot had been marked out for her at the local churchyard (the dying do not have much of a back to care what goes on behind it, though often silently contrive in imminent preparations), something of a honour in itself. And at the end several locals appeared at the burial, though in their weekday clothes they looked like curiosity-seekers, or proverbial vultures.

Christi hadn't alluded to any complaint in her conscious moments, had spoken no word that might have given Luis a clearer view as to what once had separated them and even now in impending death held them apart. So did it only exist in Luis's imagination? Because of his nature George was able to go to his study and carry on work as usual, as if nothing else in his life was happening. There was no heartlessness, Luis realised, just the result of professional rigour. At regular intervals he would leave his room, cross the small passageway, enter Christi's room and put a hand on Christi's forehead, very softly, very gently (possibly not touching the skin, Luis suspected), and Christi would smile, asleep or awake, as if recalling a now inappropriate caress or merely grateful for the shade of physical contact provided. She was in and out of sleep until the end came, but never really fully conscious, although sometimes her eyes were intensely bright, knowing. By her side when there was any suggestion of consciousness, Luis stole out for walks along the beach, solitary walks over the receiving sands, thankful that still out of season few others were to be seen (people out walking dogs would wave exaggeratedly as if encountering a lifelong friend) so she could plunge into her thoughts (thoughts that for some unexamined reason she held back from herself in the house) or seek the sanctity of her heart. In another place she would have been cautious, even satirical or such terminology, but here it seemed natural enough, called up from a part of the mind blocked out in the big city, with all its fashionable travesties.

Not being able to recall just whom she had placed her spare key with troubled her, because if there was something wrong with the one in her hand she would need to get it back. That, after all, was the basic principle behind depositing the extra key in the first place. Whoever stood beside her on the doorstep, silently immobile, could be a tenant, but so far her mind hadn't been clear enough to absorb this possibility. The screams of the gulls came in waves of lamentations, as if they were informed of her sister's coming demise or were presciently broadcasting what could only be regarded as the inevitable. At times she wished that George was with her; she felt lonely with death so close in the air, an empty, coffin-like parenthesis between every thought. She wondered why the beach, any beach, all beaches, hadn't been used for burial grounds, for the sand was soft to dig, and when the tide came in all erected headstones would naturally be wreathed with sparkling seaweed. She thought such ideas came to her as comedy relief if only because all other methods for the disposal of the dead had been readily employed and utilised. She often brought to mind scenes from a childhood shared with Christi, simple, delightful, ordinary scenes, and thought how strange and ultimately unintelligible it was that this scene today with all its spray-flecked sadness had been waiting here, destined, ineradicable, and peculiarly beautiful, forever, like the pattern on the stone she had picked up at random. No doubt George would speak of predestination or something, but if so what was this unbounded personal liberty she felt in her soul? Again, an archaic term the sea had washed up on the shore of her mind.

Yet she wasn't running away, she hadn't left her life behind, and those thoughts not entirely enthralled by the unfamiliar seascape found their way back home, irritatingly at times back to Robert, going over again, now the ground had settled, what had happened in his mind to reject her, why he had returned to living as a hermit, one of those impenetrable city recluses. Before they had become friends, lovers, he had stayed in every night, reading his library book or watching his small black-and-white television set. Or listening to that Radio 4. Those blasted pips every hour. She sighed. This sea air would have done him so much good, would have cleared up whatever wronged him; the beach walk becoming indeed the peak of her set of exercises, for the sea held more memories than were needed, and the seagulls chased them screechingly like countless sprats thrown up by the waves. Yet she had to get at what was responsible for his self-imposed isolation. She now ruled out another girlfriend because Robert wasn't the kind to chop and change indiscriminately. She wondered (and the idea was never far from her mind) if her spur-of-the-moment exercises had been successful, had reawakened buried memories and that some of these memories weren't what he might have wished for himself. She could see why he might blame her if this had happened.

At the same time, whatever he had recalled couldn't be all that bad, unwelcomed, because she knew that he continued to swim, albeit secretly from her. Or simply regardless of her knowledge of what he did or didn't do. Because if he had given her the push (and not just gone into a sort of unresponsive hibernation) why tell her? What reasons were there for keeping her informed of any of his actions? An ex-lover is farther away from you than the stranger at your elbow, she told herself, still clumsily manipulating the door key and still not properly assimilating the shadow eerily quiet next to her. Gulls screamed high above, gliding in interconnecting arcs. She periodically doubted the actual efficacy of her exercise regimes, consigned them to the basket containing many other of her whimsical ideas hatched over the years, and believed Robert had merely discovered water, but why *merely*? It was quite possible that in a previous lifetime he had won medals for it, swimming. Stood on a podium at a famous games event, gleaming cup held high in pride. The gulls cheered sharply as the image faded, more in ridicule than in praise. Discovering water for the first time could better explain Robert's obsession, his new-found passion. For hadn't swimming, particularly underwater swimming, always been compared with flying, the nearest you could get in terms of bodily liberation to actually being up there, free as a bird?

She lifted her head and shielded her eyes. The gulls made it look too easy to inspire envy though she felt pleasantly dizzy following the flight of a breakaway, a sudden maverick with ideas of its own. Few swimmers, she reminded herself, restricted themselves exclusively to one expression or another – to underwater swimming, no matter what they got from it, of having seemingly severed all links with gravitation, that strange jealousy of the earth, of in many ways returning to an earlier, less complicated state, a time when it was possible to play with the spirits, to roll and tumble with elemental forces. Most swimmers took advantage of what else could be done with water (what else it could do with you), perhaps finding diving through the air, together with the other elegant aerial configurations, an even greater freedom giving a profounder release, though of course all these could be performed underwater, intimately manipulated, for water allowed you to enter another, different time sphere. Yet from what she knew Robert swam from one end of the pool to the other in a straight line. She sensed that something strange happened in the middle, but nothing acrobatic, he didn't include the occasional joyous somersault. She loved him for his contentment with the simple, the unshowy, yet at the same time it did signify a certain lack of imagination.

Luis usually turned back when the footprints in the sand in front of her were quickly fading, although she realised that originally they had gone on much farther, had been much more adventurous. She recalled she hadn't liked Robert much at first. She couldn't trust someone who spent most of his time in his room, superiorly bored with life. There must be something peculiar about him, she'd thought. Although she didn't place a lot of value on hearsay, she had learnt from other tenants that he didn't work and spent all day at the library. Well, was he doing research? Was he looking up something that he thought hadn't received enough attention in the past? Those who accused him of wasting his time in the library never went near the place. He was known for just sitting there, staring out to space. But he looked kindly enough on other occasions. But there was a dim, half-articulated fear that he could be on some register or another. At first Luis had thought that he might be on recent release from a . . . special hospital. But when he spoke all grotesque speculations were instantly dispelled. He didn't have an accent and yet sounded as if he came from a verifiable place. When she got to know him better and he confessed (as if emerging from the closet of a secret invented history) that he suffered from amnesia she decided that he'd been involved in an unremembered road accident or something of that nature. (Later, when lovers, she secretly searched his body for telltale cicatrices.) She was happy to recall their romantic beginning, though her face clouded over at its unfathomable cessation. Had he been involved in another accident that had taken away recent memory with the rest?

Because it would cost a fortune to call out a locksmith (something that wouldn't please the landlord at all) Luis continued her struggles with the recalcitrant key, obliquely wondering why the figure by her side didn't offer any help. After his wife's funeral George went straight back to work, taking the train from Cromer to Norwich with an ordinariness that deceptively suggested Christi would be waiting for him on his return, that, as the poets deluded themselves, death had an ineffectual sting. But for a man without a religion everything had to be crowded into extinction, and he certainly believed in that. Also he'd had a good look at what moral collapse would mean for him and the memory of his wife and so recoiled sensibly, self-possessedly. For such a resolute, phlegmatic, philosophic spirit allowed him to mourn internally, without visible change to his outward self (though Luis always saw him on the sea's edge, wildly remonstrating with the pitiless Fates). Luis greatly admired this cultivated disinterest (guard yourself from the stone faces of strangers and the strange faces of stones) and sought to emulate it, but with only partial success. During her last few hours Christi had depended on him entirely, for the drugs were useless against the pain, the doctor too mean to give her the real stuff. Tormented at night, Christi looked at peace in the morning, her forehead a little furrowed, as if predicting that she would wake up in the afterlife with a headache for oversleeping. Luis would have gladly stayed on as a lowly housekeeper (at times of such deep emotion there was no job that would demean her, rather lift her up by virtue of its superficial degradation) concealing this strange inherited love that would intensify in its tended captivity.

Christi had left no will, which meant the house would go to George, for as Luis suddenly remembered (as if the protective walls having lost their purpose were bulldozed) the house had belonged to Christi, was her sister's property, was the cause of the conflict, her poignant sense of injustice. The house had belonged to their grandparents and had been left all to Christi, had been an intrinsic part of her future as a child. No reason had been given for this – this inexcusable one-sidedness (the bequest had seemed practically autocratic in itself), why one sister should receive all, the other none, nothing. No one could explain it and the grandparents hadn't figured conspicuously in the girls' lives. Luis had felt terribly wronged, the victim of a gross, unpardonable favouritism.

Children understand ownership in the adult world more than is generally imagined and to her credit Christi hadn't made much of her luck, but this hadn't assuaged Luis's disappointment, her deep resentment. The way she had dealt with this was to forget it, repress the knowledge of her sister's bewildering good fortune. Christi acted as if she had no daily consciousness of her endowment, but something had changed in her; she became a little removed from their old life together. It wasn't until both sisters were out of their teens that the house actually materialised, that Cromer became a place on the map, and Christi took possession of it. By that time Luis was unable to recognise the house as a palpable reality. Had she secretly desired the house for herself it might not have slipped away and instead become a viable part of her world. But she didn't want it for herself. She hated it for the imagined detrimental effect it had had on Christi. She wanted no part of this grotesque random conferment of gifts. But now the house was all about her, real and un-dispellable.

She thought in time George would sell up and get a flat close by the university. As a philosopher what could the material world mean to him? Like most outsiders Luis had little or no idea about philosophy and its practitioners. Yet to a certain degree she had accurately apprehended George's mentality. His occasional praise of the concrete world was a perverse affectation. Really he was a religious stranded in a godless century. He realised how much he was a product of his time and despaired of the way it had formed his mind. As a boy he liked playing with the big ideas as they came naturally to mind and didn't think himself exceptional because of them, realising that metaphysics (the word would have been strange to him then) was the domain of youthful imaginations. Now that he struggled to unravel lesser mysteries his mind still returned, if left unguarded, to the unanswered questions of his adolescence. His wife's disappearance perplexed him though he was certain that the house didn't harbour her un-ascended soul. Sometimes he found himself searching the place for her and felt embarrassed feeling Luis's eyes on him, quickly averted or dropped if he turned. When the illusion is punctured there will be a terrible sense of loss, of material forfeiture. At first George had lived in the house only because Christi had wanted it, though his camaraderie with the sea was sure and genuine. Now strangely, ironically, absurdly, Christi's love of the house had come to Luis. It had come to her with the shattering intensity of a lover's look across a room. This had happened to her on crossing the threshold, made unconsciously accessible because all her thoughts were elsewhere. Once Christi had no need of anything physical, covert love was passed to her unhindered.

With the key at last turning in the lock she felt like a safe-cracker so whoever it was standing next to her on the porch took on a more sinister aspect, though who else could it be but the postman, or a meter reader or plumber? She would take a good look once inside. Before she left for home she took one last walk along the sands with George, who was beginning to look haggard and lost, against his better intellectual judgement. There was a distraught look in his eyes, very un-stoical, as if some undisciplined part of his mind was gradually waking up to what had expired and would never return again. He was still physically strong and his thinking seemed unimpaired. Luis was surprised to know that Christi and he, George, rarely if ever strolled along the beach together, but went separately, individually, only relating their experiences, their vague but persistent impressions, later on in the evening by the fire or over the tea table. It was George's belief that they could never be alone and that by going separately along the beach – keen-eyed and self-resourceful – doubled their experience of it. People, locals, seeing them together in the centre found it difficult to regard them as man and wife because their solitary sightings hadn't connected them, were inclined to see them as brother and sister. And George had never acquired the look of a husband, his natural distance from things made him appear like a respectful brother, and in turn Christi resembled a devoted if independent pristine sister. (In shops men sometimes chatted her up and George stood by politely observing, not wanting to disturb what was, after all, a legitimate ritual.) But those who knew their real relationship were deferential, admired their quiet, distinctive, unassertive commitment to one another. Now Christi had gone and George searched for old uncorrupted footprints in the sand as semi-consciously, trance-like, he searched the darkened recesses of the house, stared for ages at her vacant chair. No one knew who Luis was, how she figured in George's life, and so speculation was rife. On the beach even the stones gossiped and sniped.

After her week was up – and it was as if she heard the curt, unanswerable click of an outgoing turnstile – Luis was ready to return to London. But her eagerness should have told her something was wrong, that the geographical orientation had taken a knock. But George, who ignored all impact, snubbed all wayward collisions, seemed in no hurry to sell the house and invited Luis to visit whenever she cared to, although this she feared could be nothing more than a conventional parting phrase. (He was quite capable of manipulating the conventional aspects of life when it suited him, found no contradiction with including the orthodox in his philosophy when the situation benefited from it.) Nonetheless she was very touched and hoped it reflected her unrevealed affection for George himself. She wondered if George would end up living alone in the house, discovering some hidden connection with it, becoming over time the local high-minded eccentric, a formidable presence in a place entrenched in a tradition of robust simple-mindedness.

On the train journey back she felt both sad and elated, watching a gentle curtain of rain fall over a succession of pastoral and then industrial scenes. At the boarding house she experienced considerable trouble getting through the front door and wondered how much this uncharacteristic ineptitude had to do with her regret at being 'home'. It didn't help matters much when Robert, who had been standing next to her in some blank-eyed, moronic stupor, rushed by and up the stairs, once the door was open, without a single word of greeting.

CHAPTER ELEVEN

Robert had never felt so nervous in his life. And this wasn't primarily because he was in a pub he hadn't been in before or because the surrounding area was antithetical to his sensibilities (he liked to think he was hard, but he wasn't; life's blows had produced in him a different kind of hardness and this wasn't the place to exploit it), but because of the project he had in mind. And this wasn't the time to examine it again, to allow his face in a kingdom of strangers to reveal its shameful calculations. The moment he gave in, let his face go in that direction, all that he had concluded and buried, repressed at the end of the iron rainbow, would be revealed on his face in a bonfire of grimaces, like a madman blowing his top again, a show he had to guard against at all costs. He took a drink of his beer to cool his burning cheeks. His fingers trembled less with such a heavy weight in his hand. Quite a change from the dandelion gravity of a wine glass. And he had almost made the mistake of asking for a glassful when first at the bar only to be warned off by a quick glance around. Not that there seemed many in tonight, but as a famous French philosopher once remarked the heavy brigade were conspicuous by their absence. Now was the time to take out a cigarette and inspire personal coolness (or what the same French philosopher would have called unflappability), but Robert didn't smoke, and it was too late to start. You just can't start enjoying a vice after having ignored it for so long. That this seemed patently untrue forced him back into his reflections, a bolt-hole he'd been secretly furnishing for some time now and from where he could obtain a certain measure of protection from the vulgar world.

* * * * *

Although Robert had started on a new artistic career with abstract painting, a drastic departure which had profoundly shaken his agent and those familiar with his previous, ultra-conservative work, he sensed the approach of the end. He was uncomfortably aware of excessive repetitiveness, a noticeable lack (at least for him) of progressively original application. He wasn't greatly disturbed by this, secretly hoped that he might return to his old realistic style, to the days when draughtsmanship had meant everything, detail, the head of the pin where the devils, the abhorrent creatures of darkness, danced. But that calmness of vision had been lost once Hilliary had walked out on him, once she had gone to live with her boyfriend, and his world had collapsed into chaos. He had thought of killing himself, but that was just an idea, a point of potential escapism the roulette wheel had stopped at before spinning on again, rejected if temporarily attractive. During that period his wife seemed to have gone off her head, completely oblivious of the pain she inflicted, that her ecstatic behaviour had over him, as slowly he fell apart. If anything, she appeared resentful that Robert perversely refused to join her in her new love, her new rapturous infatuation. John, the boyfriend, the schoolteacher, assumed an attitude of rational complacency, almost a doltish serenity. As if no sense of wrongfulness could penetrate his middle-class smugness. But at least he didn't expect Robert to get involved in Hilliary's absurd mood, her self-obliterating imbecilic euphoria. Robert just felt awful, intermittently cataleptic, gave up painting, sat up in his attic inhaling oil paint and drinking all the time. But he could never find real forgetfulness, and often his heavy drinking produced nothing but a hallucinatory lucidity of what he was afraid to confront, an exaggerated version of what he was running away from.

Only, of course, he wasn't running away. Not physically, not in a way that gave him a break from it all. He remained exactly where it had taken place, unable to find the spirit to save his life elsewhere. He was afraid to move. He thought that his calamity had lost hold of its perimeters. At first he hadn't been distressed by his wife going off to live with her lover, went on as if nothing had happened, if possible more engrossed in his work than ever. He didn't think it would last. It was just a two- or three-week fling (eternally pledged at the time but . . .) and then she would be back, and he would forgive her, genuinely forgive her. On his second bottle of wine in the evening he'd shed copious tears at the extent and quality of his compassion, his mercy. (Behind an old wardrobe in a corner of the attic he was putting down a time capsule of the period so that she would be able to read and see what had been going on during her period of excusable lunacy.) And he had no attitude towards John, her lover, saw him as a blank entity. For Robert, the schoolteacher was a one-dimensional character, not worthy of thought. But John was married, had a couple of kids and he had sacrificed this, left this life behind, to live with her, Hilliary, Robert's wife. But she didn't come back, not permanently, not outside of pretending to be worried over his well-being, dropping in unannounced, inanely grinning. Then Robert's amused tolerance turned to bewilderment and venom.

He couldn't recall when first he started to attack his canvases like a savage, when he turned against his previous commitment to realism with a vengeance, with a turbulent lust of retaliation. Once he was into it he felt he had been such a painter all his life. These displays of emotion, inner anguish, seemed natural to him, the only way to put across the kind of man he was, express his reactions to life's varied onslaughts. Looking back, he could see the violence behind his neat, precise drawings, safely locked away in the cages of his perspective-obsessed paintings. He had removed the protective enclosure of his previous work and treated (if that was the word) the viewer to the unguarded conflagration. Because his previous work had been without transitional passages the shock to some could not have been greater, and his first nights were exciting events rather than a tired affair. Over the years abstract art had become bland, impersonal, and dependable. Now Robert had reinvented what it was to be really involved again. When Hilliary had first seen his new work she'd had two simultaneous reactions: one, that he was biting off his nose to spite his face; two, that surprisingly, unexpectedly, he had made an immensely significant breakthrough, that at last he'd found the courage to reveal his inner self, what was 'stamped indelibly on his soul'.

Others mightn't have noticed it, but he certainly would, did, and finally that was all he cared about, his own sense of self-authenticity, even during a time of personal devastation – particularly during such a time, for if he couldn't regard himself as an artist what could he regard himself as? The twitching corpse his wife unconsciously wanted to see him become? So he abandoned his breakthrough, or becoming painfully conscious of the frequent restatements looked about for another means of expressing what he had to say, and found it where the others originated from, behind his eyes. He literally saw this in vague instalments before it actually focused in his mind, presenting itself as clear and unchallenged. Something that had been in progress all along, but which now had made itself visually unmistakable. This struck him as astonishing, the breakthrough of breakthroughs, but of course he hadn't been able to see it until the full picture flashed backwards illuminating each individual development, each previously unaware-of advancement. So it came both as a breakthrough and as a refreshing knowledge of all that goes to make up a breakthrough – all the usual unhonoured segments, buried under the final revelation. All that usually goes by the wall and is forgotten.

Why take the trouble to actually paint when all could be done in his head, saving much more time for what he really liked doing these days, which was to drink (a terrible admission perhaps, but not entirely unknown among artists of any generation). And by this subtle process of mental painting he could achieve some extraordinary effects. What he saw inside his head was such an improvement, such an unforeseen development, on what he could do in the laughingly real physical world – what cerebral pigment could be put into the pure, unmediated intellectual realm, that it was hard to seriously justify going on with what was obviously an outmoded, obsolete method of . . . of artistic endeavour. And wasn't this one over on Monet's last wish to be able to paint pure air itself? With the mind as his studio there were no limitations to the projects he could devise, conjure with, and all the while keeping a firm hand on the bottle. This surely was the perfect solution to Hilliary's desertion, to the pain, the agony, of a badly bruised ego, the resentment burning deep inside his soul. Certainly it seemed all physical exertion was a thing of the past when it came to postmodernistic artistic innovation. But the rage was still there, the anger, first realised if ineptly demonstrated when he had attempted to attack them both, and missed by a mile, the only damage done being that to the wall, where chips in the plaster still remained, a series of sharp gashes, irregular lacerations of a poorly executed assault. On waking sober in the morning he had been infinitely grateful for his bungling attempt, but later cursed his lack of skill, had fantasised for hours with himself as ice-cool professional contract killer, or at least someone who possessed the natural ability for this kind of thing reported every day in the newspapers. And according to mood, to accumulating glasses of wine, he continued to fantasise a cold-blooded murder of one or the other or both, construct and reconstruct an appealing episode time and again, until he could practically hear their bodies slump to the floor (as his choice of weapon progressively complicated itself), sprawled over the ground, like the much anthologised cliché of a sieve-like, bullet-riddled sack or sacks of coal. Oatmeal. Hops, etc.

For a time his mental artwork had satisfied him, had been visualised vividly enough to pass for more than the real thing, even though such cerebral canvases were virtually unmarketable. Yet like intellectual aesthetic productions were the real thing, as paintings seen in dreams are not only the real thing, but surpass in beauty and originality (and in a haunting, indecipherable autobiographical content) anything that can be produced in the waking state. Though some appeared to be uncanny prophecies of greater work yet to be painted, in galleries yet to be built, for spectators yet to be conceived. With a glass of red in hand there seemed to be no ceiling Robert couldn't paint with the most inspiring if obscure images. Robert didn't know what category this work fitted into and sometimes the two forms of fantasising overlapped with grotesque results. Strangely, the more complex his murderous fantasies became the more he seemed to recognise their plausibility, the less he regarded them as fantasies in the strict sense of the word. And finally they became for him realistic projections, blueprints for a crime. He no longer thought of the taking of a life as a great moral obscenity. In fact he thought of prematurely dispatching someone to hell (or a vast indifferent void) as a godly act. And he could see himself held up to the world as someone directly responsible for the apparent death of another person without having contempt for the system that misunderstood his motives and humiliated him. In other words he didn't see himself as getting away with it. Without any metaphysical humour intended he believed that he could live with that, a proper lawful conviction and an undisputed life sentence. Of course he would seek redemption and knew God would require profound penitence, sorrow. Robert saw himself in the prison library making certain all the books were in their proper places and once or twice a week pushing a little wooden contraption on wheels about the penitential labyrinth packed with novels for those sinners who wished to improve their spiritual condition.

Perhaps if Robert had been betrayed before (prior to his relationship with Hilliary his spontaneous trust in others had always been repaid) he would not have felt it so much, so intensely, this time (although treachery is rarely taken in one's stride). Therefore his deeply offended heart demanded reparation. And his fantasising couldn't, wasn't designed to, compensate for the affliction. He knew only true justice and justice alone could neutralise the suffering, the pain he continued to endure. Having paved the way his fantasising then retreated under the endearing fleece of immaturity. At first the thought of what had to be done was so absolute and un-negotiable that he reconsidered the idea of suicide, but again dismissed it as a fleeting gruesome shadow or saw it as being nothing but an extension of his wife's cruelty. The thought of Hilliary prodding his lifeless body on one of her visits to make sure that he wasn't letting himself go filled him with horror. Seeing the daunting prospect of going over the edge he made a concerted heroic effort and pulled himself together. At once he reduced his alcoholic intake and concentrated solely on what had to be done, what had become fixed, inevitable and irreversible in his mind. Hilliary had ruined his life and so her fate wasn't open to discussion. He felt that his suffering had given him access to a superior authority. He scraped himself free of daydreaming like a man in a jungle without anaesthetic rips off a top layer of infected skin. To do what was unchangeable he had to be exposed to the harsh, unfiltered light of reality. Though in the contemplation of what was to be done there was a fractious kernel, a secret, exquisite, subversive dream. If only all hadn't been so deceptively simple, all so straightforward . . . he knew that he must be wary of the hidden complexities, the unsurfaced ramifications that would try to make matters more intricate than they need be (he would need to employ Occam's razor sweepingly); for if he thought too long and too wearisomely there was a real danger that his imagination would overcomplicate matters, introduce irrelevant details, unplanned minutiae, better-aborted tibs and tabs, in fact difficulties that belonged to an entirely different and unrelated scenario. This had been his problem in the past, he mused unsparingly: over-elaboration.

Hilliary with her wild-eyed, euphoric happiness – Had love made her into a mystic? Did she sense something far more deeply interfused? And if so what good was this to Robert? What could it do for him, but increase his rage, exasperate his anguish? – persistently attempted to persuade him to visit them, but so far he had held out, resisted. No amount of lunatic frothing was ever going to entice him across that threshold, into that flat of theirs. That had been his righteous declaration to himself. There were principles at stake here. Now he could see his moral obligation being vastly different from before. He saw his previous impassivity as a trap he'd foolishly fallen into, a hole from which he had been manipulated into performing exactly along the lines of their desires, doing precisely what they wanted him to do in order to intensify his suffering (irrespective of any scripted strategy), to augment his pain. She had more or less immobilised him with reflected love and with spontaneous scheming. She had paid regular if impromptu visits begging him to see them, impressing on him a blind deceptive untruth, that he would be welcome, he would be embraced, his pain (self-created, of course) would be exorcised. Now off the drink and sober as a fish he had acquired an objective vision that permeated everything. A paradoxically impersonal, objective passionate vision that shot through all he saw and remembered. But he hadn't expected to be so nervous, so full of what his mother used to call the collywobbles. At this stage he hadn't expected his body to have so many previously unconfessed reservations about what he intended doing.

Although unknown, strange, intimidating, this was the pub (the art world was abundant with borderline information) where he'd been told that a gun could be had for the right money. Yet he was practically a stranger in this part of East London, that of the infamous or legendary Whitechapel. Though on seeing its dilapidated streets he'd wished he had visited it in the days when he was a broad-shouldered realist, and its sharp and angular perspectives still intrigued him. The name of the pub he'd been given was the Pelikan and he found it without much trouble – the man he'd first asked for its locality had almost guided him to it in person and seemed about to hand him over to the next geographical torchbearer when Robert politely insisted that he could probably make it unsupported. The Pelikan turned out to be a small, exhausted pub, with what appeared to be an ever decreasing clientele. The forlorn spaces between each drinker hinted at better, popular times. A woman's chair at one end of the bar and covered with a membrane of dust had given up trying to catch the eye. The dartboard had lost its wire monocle and stared starkly at the opposite wall. Behind the bar he could see a row of freakily vaporised spaces which at first he imagined were the remains of previous barmen exposed to a terrible force, but which were probably the patches of old contrivances ripped away from the surface and left at that. Then ramping up the necessary courage Robert went over to the bar and said he was after a shooter, a word he'd picked up from the television he'd been reduced to watching again. He had said this in a voice that he could easily excuse as drunken humour if need be. But after a cursory inspection the barman told him to return the next evening, tenish, which obediently he did.

The barman looked at him for a fraction of a second in recognition (he'd allot you a full second if you'd been coming in for ten years) but poured him a glass of the same stuff he'd enjoyed the night before, and then gave him five fingers. Five minutes. The barman's eyes were as big and round and white as golf balls and were on the other side of belligerence and would stay there unless you gave him any trouble. Robert nodded (he wasn't half as nervous as the night before so was in control of some non-vocal forms of communication) and sat at a small unoccupied table. The regulars appeared in their established places, although slightly moved, indicating that minuscule revolutions were in progress all the time. He noticed how occasionally glasses were lifted, cigarettes produced and lighters snapped, like autocratic fingers. Cheeks were sucked noisily in and ragged plumes of grey smoke released into the air. In what could have passed punctiliously for five minutes a smartly dressed man in his forties came in turning the kind of heads that protectively contradict a previous immediate recognition. Conversely the barman's blank expression turned to one of secretive knowing. The laborious rate at which he had been cleaning a glass speeded up, as if the man was a representative from the brewery.

'That him?'

The man asked this question without turning so that to Robert he looked like a man in a painting by Magritte. And then for a moment the whole pub turned surreal, little mysteries nestling everywhere, a sense of a bizarrely shared joke. Robert's heart thumped violently and he hoped that his abrupt severance from drink wasn't about to instigate a fully fledged hallucinatory attack. Clutching the money in his coat pocket it felt like a soggy bundle of tissues. The man turned and Robert noticed that he had one of Magritte's faces too, infinitely bland and characterless, but capable of any vile act because he lacked a conscience. In the past Robert hadn't much liked Magritte's work, thought it too polished, too facile, but now he saw what it was about: the impending brutality hiding behind the superficial, enigmatic mask. The man smiled familiarly, came over and sat at Robert's table. Was this it? Robert's palpitations seemed to morse chronically to his brain. What would happen next? But the man said nothing (exerting his authority?) and merely studied Robert in a leisurely way, as if Robert had put in an application form for a provisional regular. Then, his curiosity apparently satisfied, the man turned slightly and nodded at the door next to the expired jukebox, a door he hadn't seen before, but he already knew about the anonymity of some doors and the blatant conspicuousness of others.

'Now,' the man said categorically, standing up.

'Now?' Robert questioned, but he stood up nonetheless and followed the man, who opened the door with a key handed him by the barman, who looked contemptuously at Robert as he passed by, through the space provided by the open door.

Robert was very nervous now and realised that the nervousness wouldn't stop, calm down, for a very long time. He wasn't where he should be. He was displaced, outside of what he was accustomed to thinking of his world. And yet he knew this transfer was basically unavoidable and had to be endured. Taking regular gulps of air, he followed the man along a foul-smelling passageway and out into a dark backyard stacked with crates and barrels and planks from an unfinished carpentry job. The man stopped and now was completely covered in shadow. Like a weak ether the odour of beer was everywhere. What little light there was came from outside the gates, from an un-snooping lamp post from an indifferent constabulary.

Cold with fear, Robert thought, 'This is it, when the butt of the gun strikes my skull, and I go down, sprawled out among the dog-ends and empty crisp packets and spent condoms. How could I have been so gullible, so childishly naïve, so utterly stupid . . . ?'

CHAPTER TWELVE

Robert sat on the edge of his bed nursing his damp rolled-up towel and staring with a bewildered expression at the opposite wall. He was vaguely aware of having virtually collided with Luis on the way in and wondered now if he should have spoken to her, said a word or two, because certainly he didn't want to bring attention to himself, appear churlish, have her, or anyone else come to that, think that there was anything wrong with him. But his thoughts seemed to have built an obstruction to everyday invisible behaviour. As soon as he had an ordinary, unexceptional thought this was immediately intercepted and destroyed by another bizarre and unlikely one. His mind was always straying into alien airspace. Since he had rented his room and started thinking about his apparently non-existent past (what he sensed should be there, but remained frustratingly un-excavated) he had enjoyed access to the fundamentals of modern life. Abstract knowledge of the commonplace essentials, the nuts and bolts of survival, hadn't gone the mysterious way of his errant memory. Now with the return of this memory – confusing, unnerving, shocking as it was – he felt gradually less able to deal with what once he hardly gave a thought to. He described this to himself as gross preoccupation, the way anyone might act if obsessed with a great distracting idea. Wasn't this the origin of the 'absent-minded professor' myth? (And today anyone who could spell his middle name held a doctorate.) But really, he wasn't dealing with unearthly matters. He wasn't dealing with complex, erudite theorems. No.

What he was dealing with was the psyche-shattering enigma of being an entirely different man from the one he had believed himself to be.

Even when suffering fully from amnesia he'd had the idea of himself as a definite sort of person, even if he hadn't been able to positively articulate that idea. He had felt himself to be, intrinsically, a particular sort of man. Now all this had changed and the world was changing with it. The room looked different to him, as if he hadn't seen it for a long, long time. It looked unfamiliar as if being scrutinised by different eyes. The rolled-up towel in the crook of his arm looked strange too, as if he had picked it up outside and had been walking around with it to no ascertainable end. None of this was elevated perception, for it made him feel moronic, somehow on a lower level than the one he had been on before. And he felt peculiarly manipulated, as when he let the towel roll drop while holding on to one end so that his swimming trunks fell out, fell to the floor, seemingly slimy with the afterbirth of memory, in themselves the placenta of recollection. He reached down and picked the trunks up and squeezed tight the material so that water oozed through his fingers, a sluggish flow of miry chemicals left over from the pool. He felt sick, his stomach churning over. Why was finding out who he was turning him into a stranger? He seemed closer to who he had thought he was when he had known practically nothing about himself. In fact wasn't that the secret? When all you imagined yourself to be was gone, disappeared, there you stood in front of yourself for the very first time (outside of certain self-revelatory dreams), unmistakably. Robert stood up, laughed at himself in the shaving mirror. What did he think he was up to? He'd been in for almost twenty minutes and the lid was still on the coffee jar.

Spooning instant coffee into a mug he tried to recall what had happened to his nervous, distraught, overwrought self in the beery backyard of the pub, of the queerly named Pelikan. But just after that his mind slipped away into the dyed cotton wool of amnesia. The memory literally snapped off like a biscuit. He rubbed the back of his head with his fingers and was glad that he hadn't been struck by the gun handle, although no memory was that palpable. Why a specific memory or related concatenation of memories broke off suddenly wasn't clear, as this often occurred before he'd finished his length, pushing him semi-consciously to the surface. He could very well swim that last distance still underwater, fully conscious, aware that what he had recalled hadn't been perfectly rounded off, or rather with a feeling that the memory should have gone on (at least to a satisfactory break), not left him tantalisingly wanting. So it was no wonder that he reached the bar with a distinct feeling of beguilement. Or the lifeguard, conspicuously shorn of all unnecessary display, came to his nonplussed rescue. Mostly though, the memory or scenario of lost life came only to an end, to its abrupt conclusion, when his head came shooting up, mouth gasping for air, hands flapping miserably, and consciousness of where he was gradually returned. No, he hadn't been struck by the gun (yet) that he was attempting to purchase criminally, unlawfully (how one desires above all the past to be free of misconduct), but there had been a sense of a partial conclusion (some natural interlude in the darkness of the backyard) as he broke the surface. As if the water had the power to create a tangible ceiling when conditions were right, something quite different from ice and other crystalline solids. For a while Robert had felt dazed, stupefied, staggered back to his cubicle under the suspicious eyes of the lifeguard.

And what penetrating introspection or self-punishing self-examination went on in that cubicle. He clicked in a couple of sweeteners, added a measured amount of powdered milk that settled like an unsinkable island before slowly dissolving. He stirred reflectively and later took a tentative sip. The idea that he had intended to commit murder, was going through one of the stages leading up to it, astounded him. All the lucid reasoning that had gone through his head in the recall, the memory, now had all the horrific clarity of a nightmare. But how could he doubt what was irrefutably part of the pattern? He could feel the memory and others alive in his brain as if he thrust the power of recollection into a tin of worms. You picked one and it wriggled and then the squeamishness you might feel about leaving your actual time and place vanished. Yet no more than when he had asked himself could he feel love for his wife, Hilliary, could he say now that he truly hated her, felt enough destructive ill-will towards her to wish her dead, even for her betrayal of that uncertain love. And was it really another kind of question to ask himself if he could really kill her? To see her so clearly was to deny all else but the truth of her objective existence. And the more he thought of her the more she would fade like an image in a dream and it was time again to plunge the recalling hand into the tin of worms. He wriggled his fingers in front of his face as if a memory could be conjured up without first going for a dip and then sat on the edge of the bed to look with increased focus at what he already had.

One of the troubles about love was that you could never see what partners saw in each other. You could make certain *assumptions*, but unless you were close to both of them in turn you could never really understand the individual or mutual attraction. For the life of him he couldn't see what Hilliary saw in John, the schoolteacher. He couldn't even begin to imagine what happened in her heart and mind when she saw or thought about him. Unless of course the secret of love was that one of the partners must be so vacuously composed that the other and more powerful partner could project into him or her any romantic fantasy they had been slowly or scrupulously constructing on a conscious or unconscious level or a combination of the two. Outsiders perceived no change (they weren't doing the investing), but the partners had access to new and shining worlds. Robert felt nothing for John, he was peculiarly outside the equation, having no discernible identity. And yet if Hilliary was to die so must John, the schoolteacher, for it would be an insult to her memory to let him go on living, even if death might grant him a personality he hadn't himself achieved in life. Though each time Robert consulted these memories they came out differently or occupied different positions, refused to appear fixed in exact spatial sequences. It was as if after a while no memory could be settled, but quivered in the corner hole before going down or bouncing away or being plucked up and put down in a spot seemingly incongruous – distressingly or exhilaratingly absurd.

What also bothered Robert was that if – and these *if*s stuck out of memories like harpoons from whales – if he had been something of a successful artist why was he unknown to himself, so to speak? After all, he read the Sunday newspapers and listened to the art programmes on the radio. Of course there were many admirable minor artists who received little public exposure, who went on doing their own thing or added, practically anonymously, to whatever breakthrough was in progress at the time. Also, of course, there were those artists who remained entirely unknown during their own artistic ministry and only came to light, sometimes to stunning illumination, after they had gone. Such fascinating and frequently misunderstood artists were all part of the aesthetic legacy, though in truth Robert failed to see the good of posthumous fame. The prospect of future recognition could well act as a consolation to an artist uncelebrated in his day yet (and accuse Robert of philistinism) he couldn't see any artist working painstakingly towards a day when he himself wouldn't be around to receive well-deserved praise, respect (overflowing bouquets). That might well be the fate, the predisposition, of a messiah, an avatar, a prophet, even many an unrecognised guru, but not an artist. Suddenly Robert got to his feet, a frisson of martyrdom travelling up his spine.

He washed the coffee mug under the tap and then wiped it with a piece of cloth that wasn't quite a tea towel. He screwed the lid of the small jar of cheap coffee on properly (it had been slightly askew), reflecting that as a working artist in his previous lifetime he would have no doubt possessed a coffee percolator, coffee mill and a good supply of rich beans, might well have been in the habit of visiting a select coffee shop each morning or afternoon on the dot, his customary chair and table waiting. A pungent aroma stabbed his nostrils at the surrogate memory. Strange. It appeared material possessions remained in the background of a recollection unless specifically called forth by a memoriser. He picked up his swimming trunks and pegged them drippingly to a small line running over the draining board, knowing he would use them again, that his visits to the pool weren't over. His stomach cramps had eased a lot since he'd given in and gone there again, after the initial soothing submergence (as if the fire which had engulfed him had been extinguished in a single cloud of sizzling steam), but he feared they'd be back if left too long, the aches and pains and the intolerable anguish, organs he couldn't even name screaming out for mercy. Yet hounded by a conscience never lost in time and space he wondered if any self-knowledge was really worth all the trouble, the torment involved. Hadn't he been given the opportunity to start again? Perhaps it was better – morally superior – to stay away from the pool and manfully endure all they – he could throw at himself. Stoically endure the withdrawal pains, the mental confusion, the faceless gauntlet he was forced to run each morning when he woke up without a past.

He went over to the window and looked down at the opposite row of backyards. What was it about backyards that made the world appear stuck in a permanent afternoon? No matter how chronically your life was showing up, there was an irresistible desire to know how things would turn out, if you could. He could if he wanted speed up the process, at least on an imaginative level, simply by sketching out a number of plausible possibilities, shuffle them about, juxtapose them, contrast them, even have them overlapping, and then as it were press your pen down over a particular network, trace the pattern revealed, and read that off as fate or predestination or personal history. For wasn't this working along a superimposed track that gave validity to abstract destiny? These were the sort of thoughts that came to him at the library, when he laid down his book and stared at the light streaming through the windows, falling over the shelving where conceivably could be found that esoteric volume of his dreams, the book that would change his life. Then, if only he had known it properly, he had lived in glorious forgetfulness, his past erased, in a state of grace. Had he known about the strange power of the pool in advance (the unholy wings of the lesser gods) he would have stayed away from its waters, repelled any urge to go under and dredge up the mystery of a life well left alone. But all that had been hidden from him and in truth he hadn't taken Luis's exercises seriously. How could he? She was an eccentric excitable woman, vulnerable to peculiar ideas. She was really an artist looking for a new, unconventional set of tools to express herself. And like all artists she had a special relationship with a younger, immature, creative self. If he hadn't become so hypnotically distracted he would still be enjoying an intimate friendship with her.

As if coffee had the power to re-stimulate memory, Robert felt lured across the room to make another mugful, although strictly speaking he wasn't due for another caffeine buzz for an hour or so. The idea had been developing in his mind, slowly at first but with some force now, that if he changed pools the memories might not continue to return. Indeed, had Luis initially taken him to a different pool would anything that had happened have taken place? But he recalled during his week's water fast feeling pulled from different, diverse directions, though the direction of the most powerful force was never in doubt. But he wondered if he would get the next instalment if he jumped in anywhere, in an unfamiliar pool farther out. Yet he knew that the pool he went to had a character and a magic all its own. Still, the question persistently arose, if he could go to any pool would he get what he was getting now or was there something specifically and incontrovertibly related to the way his world was working out, unfolding as it was? Similarly, was it safe to speculate that what he experienced, far from being unique – exclusive, solitary – was that of many, possibly numberless, others? None of which had any knowledge of each other (the experience felt distinctly un-sharable), would never know or encounter each other. Robert had what amounted to a practically infallible instinct that what was happening to him was a definite one-off. Certainly there could be other ways of regaining a lost or dysfunctional memory, but the method by which his were retrieved wasn't to be repeated.

Irritated, Robert took his coffee mug over to the sink to wash it out, but he had turned the tap on too forcefully and the water splashed out of the mug and over his shirt front and he recoiled, as if from an acid attack. This menacing aspect of water should have vanished, he told himself, since he had returned to the pool, but it fearfully lingered on. But he was still afraid of it, this deceptively innocuous translucent liquid. (Just before climbing out of the pool a little earlier on he'd cupped his hands and looked at the rather dull, lifeless water he'd scooped up. What had he expected to see? A weird, semi-invisible, tadpole-like life? Water teeming with scaled and plated creatures, exiles from a passing comet?) He cleaned and put the mug back in its place, determined to adhere to the common routines he'd decided on when he'd first moved in, when he'd darkly, groggily, unsteady with nothing in the past to back him up, gone through the motions of renting the room. Acting alone with abstract knowledge and a little recent memory was like making do with a handout, a small gratuity for services unremembered. The landlord had seemed curiously amused, but prepared to deal with all types, though at one time seemed on the verge of turning him away, had not amnesia given Robert a frank, inoffensive air. Now he had developed a genuine affection for the room, though sometimes he hated it or even dreaded it. He had noticed when drying himself in the cubicle that the aches were already returning, that his muscles were starting to stiffen, that he had a premature yearning for the water, felt an inexplicable longing to go back in, something he hadn't done before. He sat down on the edge of the bed again and started to massage neck and arms, rolled up his trouser legs and kneaded his calf muscles that had started giving him stabbing pains. He doubted very much if he would ever hold out a week again, even if he came up to date with his memory. With the painful throbbing along his spine and the sort of sorrowing about his heart, he wouldn't be surprised if he was back in the pool the very next morning. At least (and regardless of the memory culled) he would achieve some degree of alleviation from his suffering, which he imagined would more than perceptibly increase overnight. But how long would this go on for? If his lost memory successively returned to the point of his amnesiacal attack and then started to darken over he had only a hellish future of going round in endless circles to look forward to.

CHAPTER THIRTEEN

'I'm a part-time amanuensis' – this was the first time she'd used this word and thought she was being very daring using it on a first date – 'and privately I devise exercise regimes for the rich and famous.' Luis spoke the last part of this sentence in high mock seriousness, lifting her drink to scarlet lips and letting escape (not for the first time) a look of disgust at the trendy interior of the pub she was in, The Moral Outrage. She didn't know why she'd come here – well, she *knew*, but could that really be the reason? Curiously, the periodic permissible immoral performances (and that's what they were, allowable acts of naughtiness) were beginning to make her uncomfortable. She knew from experience that if this continued (and why should there be any selective letting-up?) the drink, far from making her feel more relaxed (indiscriminately accepting) and at home, would make her increasingly satirical and (what was that priceless word rarely heard these days but included in her grandmother's top ten?) bolshy. But for all The Moral Outrage's silly affectedness she couldn't stay in her room (and so many other pubs were just clones of this mindless abomination) and all her friends were married or preparing for divorce, the second happiest day of their lives. Not far off a woman's shrieky voice used expletives in the way a forebear's conversation would have been salted with bon mots or foreign words. She had no ear for swear words' explosive wrath, but found them silly and rude, like a child's idea of wickedness. A little earlier on a man had pulled down his zip and urinated into a special pint pot obtainable from the barman only on request and a glitzy woman had climbed on to a table and had flashed her knickers to a monotonous handclap. Obviously more had come before and was still yet to come.

'I'm not sure I know what an amanuensis is,' Terry said, with that perfect, playful pronunciation of someone in no doubt at all as to the word's definition.

Terry was the man Luis had come into the pub to find, only of course she hadn't known in advance exactly who he would be. Now while assessing his merits she was beginning to have grave doubts about her ability to make friends in this way. Surely she had left this meat-market scenario behind years ago? Yet in truth after her failure with Robert she had lost considerable confidence in her ability to make friends, form lasting relationships. The episode with George in Cromer seemed too rare and isolated to help restore any lost credibility on this very important level. But she couldn't allow herself to turn into a stay-at-home, someone jumping at every slam of the front door, frantically decoding snippets of conversation drifting along the passageway. The look in Robert's eyes that day had, candidly, frightened her. How long had he been standing next to her on the porch without saying a word? Of course she had been in a state too, but . . . But he had looked worse, ill, reverted to a stranger, like ill people do. That's what any affliction was, she thought, the annulment of intimacy. She looked Terry full in the face and saw that like any man trying to make out with a woman he appeared never to have been ill in his life.

'It's a secretary who does her boss's bagwash,' Luis said, delighting in the obsolete vernacular.

When he had approached her Luis had instantly summed Terry up as a fashionable bohemian. A modern, shabby grandee. But he was more folksy than the other males in The Moral Outrage. He wore faded corduroy trousers and a dog-eared paperback poked out of a pocket, student-like, of an unkempt jacket. But he had on polished, expensive shoes, a secret statement about hidden prosperity not meant to be too difficult to perceive. It was, Luis decided, the kind of progressive threadbareness that is meticulously cultivated. Not pretentiously, but because Terry hated stylishness (or had a love–hate relationship with it). And he thoroughly disliked giving the impression that he had taken any significant trouble over his appearance, though she knew that true tattiness was in need of constant repair. This must have been the general semi-conscious perception of those whose image was less complicated for he received no adverse lingering looks or unflattering remarks behind his back. Luis knew that he hated The Moral Outrage as much as she did, and that he was clever enough, psychologically inclined, to convert that hatred, temperamental revulsion, into affability, or plain indifference. Luis though really despised herself for being here, in this brainless bordello of cheap icons. Oversized organs, internal and external, decorating the walls. The drinks she could take, but she despised the expected arousal of being exposed to a multiple murderer's psychotic arrangement of brutally dismembered body parts.

'Bagwash?' Terry sounded amused. 'You sound like a gritty poet rather than a methodologist.'

A what?

'Actually, I'm doing a rather interesting experiment at the moment,' Luis told him, while watching with extreme boredom as a woman of massive size whipped out a breast from a low-cut dress much to the bug-eyed appreciation of a semicircle of male admirers, 'but alas there's such a thing as client confidentiality.' She wondered if the infantile indecencies going on around her were responsible for her current recourse to archaic expressions. She recalled doing something like this as a child on the school bus, loudly using posh words when the kids from the rough estates were getting too vulgar at the back. Sending down messages of unintelligible superiority. She liked Terry for taking no notice of their fatuous exhibitionisms (although of course he could not be oblivious of them), for being above the puerile depravities of The Moral Outrage. There was no one interesting enough at the office to go out with, and being part-time she was often cruelly treated as a non-person, someone not entirely integrated, left out of their more intimate involvements (as if being an 'agency girl' meant that she had no definite identity), left out, even, of their jokes, those weird, self-evolving facetious humorous chains, so bewilderingly self-referential. Still, they were capable of compassionate gestures. The fact was that if she really believed herself talented, skilful, clever enough to effectuate a significant breakthrough . . . Oh, was this the best she could do in putting it to herself . . . ? Then for a while she had to endure a certain amount of isolation, misunderstanding, years, perhaps, of personal misery. For that's the way people sometimes live who have original ideas, who have something of real value to express. This she was only just coming to believe in and not dismiss or denigrate her ideas as whimsical notions unfit to be taken seriously. And this was when she had problems with her own authenticity. Because she had nothing in the way of academic qualifications, except for a secretarial diploma, she was apt to feel slightly inferior when contemplating the actual projected effectuality of her developing scheme. A small voice she could not altogether suppress called her a fake. That she was trying on something she had no business to try on. And what had gone wrong with Robert was less than encouraging. She continued to dream of getting back with Robert, straightening things out, and then pushing ahead afresh. It wasn't all that unlikely Robert had something to contribute from his own experience, something she hadn't previously considered. If only he would let her know what he had come to see and understand! Then what a team they would make, she told herself, both professionally and . . . romantically. Or would she just have to come to terms with the fact that she would never know the details of the secret trysts Robert made with his past underwater?

'Client confidentiality . . .' Terry nodded. 'I always say, nothing you say leaves this room. Nothing. Whatever you say is perfectly safe with me.'

He had told Luis that he had recently qualified as a

psychotherapist. He occupied an office in a building owned and cared for by a group of other psychotherapists. He loved his work. It was always what he had wanted to do. Before he'd had many types of work, but had never found any real satisfaction, never felt that he was doing anything of real importance. But it had been just this restlessness that finally brought him to an exploration of the mind. Having for years submitted himself to self-analysis (all those dreary walks through wind-driven streets, sitting for hours in gloomy cafés, staring sightlessly at indecipherable exhibits in death-dealing museums) he had gotten himself 'looked into' professionally, had his past turned out, the bones of past tyrants tagged, docketed, and definitively identified. Superficially no change had taken place, he looked to others (friends, if they had survived the ordeal) just the same as he had before, but inside he was transformed. Real knowledge of his own past had changed him from the depressed moron or harassed, shadowy nobody he had been, to a self-determining individual, a man to be reckoned with because he successfully reckoned with others. Other psychoanalysed people. Luis had been very impressed, and yet still she perceived some integral uncertainty in Terry's character, something she couldn't find the right words to express.

'Many of those who follow my exercises' (poetic licence helped Luis to see a bright successful future for her system) 'end up in the drink,' (she allowed the colloquialism to evoke its own images) 'so each must have an individual course of exercises specifically . . .' She let her words fade, hearing the rhetorical tone of discourse entering her voice, that talking-to-yourself inflection, unappetising for whoever you are with.

Over at the bar, on top of it in fact, a couple were simulating sexual intercourse with a chorus of exaggerated grunts and passionate groans. Was this the literal climax at The Moral Outrage? Luis asked herself. The act itself still beyond the controlled inhibitions of this grotesquely artificial environment. Feeling a vague relief that the two involved in dry or pretended sex were of different sexes themselves was the only shock Luis received, speaking a lot for a superannuated code of behaviour she hadn't completely rid herself of. What a contrast all this was to her recent experience of the reinvigorating naturalness of the seaside. (Although what could be more profane than a fish? Specially some of those weirdos lower down. She dreaded to know what *they* got up to.) She was of course only just back, and the smell of the sea was still in her nostrils, the bumpy tread of beach stones still under her shoe, the wind still dishevelling her hair fashionably. Her ears held the memory of George's voice, deep, rich and infinitely wise. How terrible it must be alone in that house, even with such original thoughts. She could see now that any special look he gave her was due to a family likeness she shared with Christi, that her surmised love was nothing but a romantic illusion, conjured up by such a ravishing change of environment. By the sea people fell in love with dreams, figments of their imaginations, hybrid ghosts from the past.

'In therapy a good ducking is often thought to be the *first* step to a successful drying out,' Terry said, elbows on the table like a truck driver relaxing at his favourite café. It was strange, Luis thought, how self-knowledge deluded you into a false affinity with the proletariat. Seeming to intuit her perception Terry removed his arms from the table and dusted non-existent leather patches. Was this one of those jokes aimed at a wider, unseen audience? She wondered if Terry would agree to have a word with Robert, or would Robert need to avail himself of psychotherapy, consent to certain procedures? Ideally, another swimmer would make the best counsellor, she thought, someone who would understand the fascination of underwater swimming. Then again the best course of action might be just to leave him alone. After all, some people like being on their own – brooding, gloomily introspective, and a temporary stretch of freedom means nothing at all – though she couldn't forget how happy he had seemed, looked, sunnily reacted, when first he'd set out on her exercise regime, his face glowing with the corona of a true aspirant, regardless of the fact (she was no fool, even in love) that he had been principally doing it for her. He had become a different man, loving, caring, sensitive, full of healthy, outdoor life. She had drawn him out of his shell. And at a time when she had visualised her exercises as the product of a spontaneous whim, a series of quirks, making them up, or drawing them in, as she went along, not really seeing any significant relationship before she sensed a strong pattern emerging, a vigorous familial connection emerging. . . . Strangely enough it wasn't until Robert had shown signs of weakening that she had started to take her intuitions seriously. At about the same time he disturbingly took the decision to retreat inside himself again. When he had suddenly and tragically relinquished all the progress made until then.

'I've found that in some of my specifically designed exercise programmes' (Luis thought that to appropriate a feasible occasion prior to the actual inauguration of her future method wasn't a crime) 'an individual will get stuck at an unforeseen stage. They will lose the will to complete the course. They will suddenly take a negative attitude towards . . .' And she went on investigatively, trying to hold Terry's eye, although it was slippery, perhaps taking a peripheral interest in an amoral demonstration now in progress, or about to reach a quasi-raunchy conclusion. Whatever, Luis couldn't see The Moral Outrage staying in business much longer with this kind of counterfeit impurity, this kind of sham abandonment. Unless of course it was because their patrons were unable to take the real thing in public and this sort of childish rudeness really revealed their old-fashioned pathetic rectitude, their unconscious adherence to scruples long mouldering in the grave. It occurred to Luis then that she herself was guilty of not completing the 'course'; that, or the course as such, terminated in the pool. This was something she hadn't given much thought to before, had automatically assumed there to be many more stages left to the burgeoning course. But it was a fact that after having introduced Robert to water, so to speak, further athletic ideas (come everyday improvisatory athletic techniques) had stopped dropping out of the sky.

'There are ways to rekindle their interest,' Terry replied, in a ludicrous German SS accent.

He was a very clever, intelligent, peculiarly presentable man, but a terrible mimic. She laughed. She put the tip of her finger into her drink and pressed it against his lips. From the look in his eyes the effect was electrifying. She hadn't regretted the absence of ideas, was grateful for the pause, as their rational translation could be fatiguing. She could see now that she had considered this as a natural or even inevitable suspension, that she had concocted in and for herself something like writer's block to deal with the crisis (afraid that otherwise brilliant, irrevocable ideas would descend into the void) to get around the snag that was Robert's unexplained disconnection. She could hardly encourage ideas to continue fructifying when her faculty to discern them, her ability to actually *see* them, was seriously impaired, even rescinded. Paradoxically, she wanted to retain control over what she no longer had any direct association with. On another level, that the already received and cultivated ménage of ideas should terminate with water seemed eminently reasonable. If all life had initially crawled out of the bubbly swamp (life as she knew it, life she had no trouble in recognising), as contemporary wisdom asserts, then what better place than a modern swimming pool for it to end, or rather take its next significant advance, at least according to Luis's methodology? When she got around to writing it all down she would seek expert advice on appropriate terminology.

Catcalls and whooping told her that something challengingly corrupt was making headway in some conclave of the pub though it barely aroused her. For again she saw the revealed symmetry of her ideas streak across her inner eye, was enthralled by their proportion and disclosed perfection. Her eyes were beautifully wide and guileless and Terry moved closer across the table thinking that this was the time to look into their shining depth and so catch a glimpse of that soul Jung wrote so eloquently about. But Luis blinked and the vision was temporarily obscured.

'It's always a personal disappointment when a client fails to go the full length, complete therapy,' Terry said. Then he added: 'I still have a lot of work to do on myself.'

Luis nodded sympathetically while continuing her own reflections. Previously she hadn't taken much interest in religion or had contemptuously dismissed it, blaming it for all the world's ills. Though as a schoolgirl she had been impressed by pictures of prophets who had received profound instruction from above and then went on to disseminate this to the masses, often at great danger to themselves. She recalled their long white fatherly or grandfatherly beards with affection and nostalgia. Today, she realised from the Sunday newspapers, academics who weren't religious themselves but took an interest in the history of religion regarded the biblical patriarchs as inspired poets, communicating the Word of Truth. Though others still said that they were divine conduits. Or conduits of the divine. It could get all very confusing and circular at times. Luis thought that anyone in the modern age with an original message to communicate could be considered in the lineage, as a genuine channel – even a West End librettist. Why not? Even an otherwise empty-headed yob spraying seemingly obtuse or meaningless sentiments on the walls of an underpass. Who could say who was deserving of such a memorable gift? She herself had never expected to be so blessed, endowed. She had never dreamed of acquiring her own uniquely individual voice. She quickly finished her drink and had little trouble in accepting Terry's kind offer of a refill. Swimming, she mused, was obviously the apotheosis of her method, of her progressively unveiled programme. Curiously, Robert's suffering from the water, his distractedness, his apparent disorientation, had to be his purification, his spiritual cleaning. This of course was the malady of his amnesia coming out, an incommunicable struggle that he was heroically engaged in alone. Anticipating the future course structure Luis could see that complete with the knowledge and strength derived so far a client would be expected to go it alone, finally, to tackle the last passage blindfold. To walk unaided, unassisted, free, unencumbered, for the first time. Then, feeling her left leg go numb, a lifelong undiagnosed disorder, Luis wondered if she wasn't getting above herself a bit.

'Shall we change venue?' Luis suggested, though not wishing to sound forward.

The theatrical licentiousness was beginning to give Luis a headache. Terry, who hadn't personally remarked on the antics of The Moral Outrage, agreed (possibly the frolics were no more disturbing than the average erotic fantasy of one of his clients, an animated voluptuous frieze he had conditioned himself to analyse coolly) and outside the pub Luis found the night streets a welcome change. Still relatively early, the streets were deserted and quiet, waiting for the real spew-out, the synchronised micturition in a thousand darkened doorways. Yet already black police vans stood waiting on street corners, like macabre ice-cream vans. The ghouls attracted by a sub-audible theme tune. Elderly people out walking dogs regularly stared over their shoulders with fearsome eyes. Luis and Terry held hands, that sudden, extraordinary intimacy that seems to have no palpable or even psychological transition. They walked by the swimming pool, where so much had happened for Robert and for which Luis continued to have a peculiar affection, although she had never experienced its secret power. At night, unlit, it appeared almost superfluous. She wanted to tell Terry the whole story, but where would she start? And what kind of story was it that she had to tell? For Terry it was just another in a long series of not very memorable buildings. It would die unlisted. He had been a keen swimmer as a boy, but had all but lost interest as he grew older. He had an excellent retentive memory and before he had become a psychoanalyst had imagined himself in showbiz as a Memory Man, recalling on stage untold mundane facts, dates, events, for an audience easily amazed. Luis wondered if the swimming pool should get a special mention when she came to write her course. If she should employ an illustrator to produce an image of the building to go on the front of the course books. A little simplified facade. There were so many things to think about, she thought. Even the typeface to be used would require much reflection.

'I live nearby,' Luis said. 'Can I entice you back for a coffee?'

Terry smiled and squeezed her hand. Although they had been walking in a directionless-like way she now felt as if she was guiding a child through the lonely, uninhabited streets. Their conversation – fragmentary, discursive, musical – flew about their heads like lovebirds, though they came from a different aviary than those released by Cupid's arrow. Terry was surprised to discover the semi-dilapidated street Luis lived on; from her voice he had imagined something a little more upmarket. But Luis's reconstructed accent had really outstripped the reconstruction of her environment. Not that she cared; she wasn't a great reader, but could easily see herself as a poor scholar, an impoverished mature student.

Then, as those farcical coincidences occur, Robert was on his way down the stairs as Luis was showing Terry up into her room. He stopped, frozen on the step, half in shadow, breathing rapid, hoarse. 'So, she does have another man,' he thought, the double betrayal striking deep. He stood still for a very long time, not really caring if he'd been seen, standing entirely immobile, like a soldier who had fallen asleep on duty. And he did feel on duty. Getting even a part of your memory back puts you in the ranks again. But a key turned in a door can break any spell and when Luis closed her door Robert continued his interrupted passage outside.

CHAPTER FOURTEEN

'I hope you will find this to your entire satisfaction,' Robert said, falling unwillingly into the diction of a nineteenth-century narrator (it was of course the nerves).

He put the wad of notes into the man's hand. It went uncounted, unaffectedly unnoticed into the man's inner coat pocket. Robert had been prepared to haggle, but he had become too agitated, hardly knew where he was, and it was only the pungent smell of beer and some other aroma that he couldn't identify that gave him a sense of actual, tangible place. A breeze came over the wall of the backyard and touched his hot forehead like a sliver of ice. He felt insanely grateful. The smartly dressed man had already given him the gun, which Robert allowed his eyes to scan only briefly before he put it into his coat pocket, as if uncertain about committing to memory the full reality of it. Now, peculiarly, it seemed as if the man had been willing to accept almost anything for it. Or he thought that an unmistakable novice would invariably overvalue it, pay much more than was necessary, than an unarmed professional would consent to pay. When the man had pocketed the cash without comment Robert felt the spirit of bartering rekindled, but it was too late. As if in a gesture of consolation the man handed him a little box of shells, bullets. In an unexpected, carefully articulated voice the man said he should *rehearse* first of all and in an *isolated* area before . . . But there was nothing after *before*.

Safe in his attic, in his studio, Robert sat on a stool in front of the easel and looked at, examined, the gun. Like the word *fuck* that never loses its force no matter how excessively used, a gun never loses its deadly power no matter how excessively seen – on television, in newspapers, in certain backstreet shops. And Robert felt that he was holding a concretised expletive. And the gun was a terrible rude word waiting to explore in terror and shock those in range to death. All the way home he had been conscious of nothing else but the gun in his pocket, and it had been a great effort to bridle an urge to reach up and touch or pat what he imagined to be a conspicuous bulge at his chest. Like most law-abiding people he knew absolutely nothing about guns, and it could be said that their proliferation as an image on television or the cinema had only helped to dangerously fantasise their existence, making them incredibly deadly and mockingly harmless. But Robert was informed enough to realise that the gun he had miraculously purchased was a revolver rather than an automatic. The bullets snuggled into a colony in the cup of his hand, their snouts clicking together, when he took them out of their box. With a dry mouth he thought they were unutterably beautiful. He stroked them with a forefinger and their smooth, metallic bodies excited him. Then skilfully, confidently, he loaded the chambers and spun the wheel. No toy he'd had as a child had ever led him to believe that this could be his. Robert thought that his profound appreciation of the weapon had gained him immediate intimacy with it. But what had been the isolated area the man had spoken of? Since Hilliary had left him he had been surrounded by such isolated areas. His world had become a fake neighbourhood where policemen and old ladies jumped out of doorways to surprise him and then disappeared again.

Taking aim he squeezed the trigger and a hole opened up in the opposite wall. On one side his neighbours were on holiday and on the other the attic was used only for storage. So if he practised a little this would be the usual backfire noise, until the police called and he went down and answered the door with the sort of innocent face only a man staring at a blank canvas for decades could muster. He fired again and the sound of the shot drilled into his ears and left him temporarily deaf, then ringing like the elfin bells of tinnitus.

The following evening after having spent the day painting at extraordinary speed a double portrait of Hilliary and John, the schoolteacher (in a rough parody of Gainsborough), Robert got ready for more potshot malarkey. Though in his mind there was no nonsense about it, but a genuine rehearsal for the real thing. He would have them voodooed first, a magical preparation for their inescapable nemesis. While he didn't want to waste more 'slugs' than he could replace – and he knew that under no circumstances would he be returning to that grubby, claustrophobic pub – he realised that in the end the contemplated act would require no more than the one loaded barrel. He would not be reloading the gun as they groaned and moaned because of an incompetent execution. There would be no incompetent execution. *Execution*. The word echoed in his mind, endorsing his preternatural sense of being appointed from above. He had no option but to be the agent of retribution.

Several cracks and the painting resembled an over-elaborate scorecard on a shooting range. Although he was virtually a believer or new convert of sympathetic magic it would be a strange let-down, he thought, and a squandered exercise to find them both dead due to mysterious causes. This kind of thing could only work face-to-face if their sins were to be absolved and the anguish of Robert's heart eventually appeased. For in the act of seeing himself as an avenging angel he had started to feel for them spiritually, for their unavoidable and dreadful suffering in the next world if cleansing for their crimes hadn't arisen in this. Almost from the moment the gun had sunk into his pocket Robert had conceived himself as a blameless, disembodied spirit, only partially physical, only partially of this world. There was a tremendous lightness about him, and this wasn't just the wine's doing. He woke up in the morning with this inexplicable sense of lightness, as if he'd been translated into a gravity-less dimension. Instead of the traditional hangover, his head seemed to float above the pillow like a helium sphere. His feet felt peculiarly ungrounded. What else could he be but the emissary of divine reckoning? Therefore, he was able to phone them, to sound genuinely sincere, benevolent, even humble, in arranging an evening together, something Hilliary had desired for a long time, since her betrayal (only of course she didn't call it that, since her departure, and to which, John, the schoolteacher, parroted in concurrence). Robert was able to sound genuine because he was genuine. He had convinced himself that he was on a mission sanctioned by a Higher Order.

'Another slice, Rob? You don't seem to have been looking after yourself,' Hilliary fussed. 'Not letting yourself go, are you?'

Robert said that what he had on his plate was sufficient for the time being. But he wouldn't object to his glass being refilled. John, in what appeared to Robert as a rare gesture of autonomy, gestured to one of the two bottles on the table. Even as an objective discharger of the Truth, Robert still hated the schoolteacher. That he couldn't even begin to imagine what Hilliary saw in him (sight through her eyes was forever closed to him) obviously meant that he had hidden depths, endearing traits, cute mannerisms. Apart from appearing vaguely affable the schoolteacher was yet to reveal much of himself, as if he felt his position established well enough that nothing was required of him, but for the occasional smile to indicate that he had appreciated a witticism or comprehended a political point. Not that Robert was steering the conversation in that direction (though the cuckold by virtue of his profound humiliation is usually allowed to direct the flow of talk). Hilliary though wasn't aware or feigned ignorance of this unwritten privilege, seeming intent in determining what topics were touched on. Certainly she had no interest in an intricate dissection of a failed marriage. She wanted to talk about art (which rudely excluded John from the talk), but thought Robert's latest breakthrough into mental art some kind of joke. She laughed wildly, but on reaching the bland wall of Robert's expression her laughter turned into hysterical giggles, and then nervous silence. She said it might have possibilities after all.

'I usually go out for my evening meal,' Robert lied. Although in truth he had been going out a lot recently.

After putting away a couple of bottles of cheap red in the evening in front of the box he would struggle into an old paint-flecked coat and make his fairly steady way (he rarely lost control until he reached a zenith of intoxication and even then still retained a formidable degree of equilibrium) up the road to where a row of Indian restaurants stood. Finding himself in one or another and imperially commandeering a table for himself, ordered lavishly a carafe or two while the nosh was getting ready. He became well known, appreciated, tolerated, almost liked. Treated like an eccentric Englishman. Only occasionally did he aim his frustration, his contempt, at other customers, who he thought were godforsaken, vacant-minded morons whose candlelit conversation revealed them to be morally deranged. Ticked off by amused waiters he rarely got into a fight. Perhaps because anyone who behaved like this could only be a tough guy, someone in the dangerous, unpredictable class of the rhetorical, disaffected, lyrically hearted hardman. Apart from such disappointing forays Robert seldomly had anything more substantial than a couple of small pork pies procured from the corner shop he visited daily for his wine supply.

'That's very sensible of you,' Hilliary said, amazed, as if she thought that in her wake he'd been eating out of dustbins. 'Don't you think so, Johnny?'

The schoolteacher made some sort of unintelligible noise and Robert smiled into his wine glass. It wasn't for the excesses of civilisation that people such as himself were intermittently sent off to put things right. When an ordinary man felt himself infused, propelled, by a superior power, felt the unambiguous inrush of energy from another, higher realm, to carry out a commission essential to the maintenance of rational, enlightened morality. He could feel this power now, an electricity travelling his veins, an undeniable bliss of body and soul. His vision clouded over and then became extraordinarily clear, vivid. How this common chair on which he sat ridiculed, mocked, his authority, that up till the very last moment must remain hidden, undercover. He picked up his glass and took a modest sip. Before leaving home he had finished off two bottles to nourish him for the journey and confrontation. But far from making him oblivious to what was going on at the table, he was sharply aware of his treacherous wife exchanging conspiratorial glances with Johnny boy, knew that they had worked out a secret code to communicate defamatory observations. Of course they regarded him as a fool and it was all part of his disguise that they should continue to think him one. Any of his remarks were so subtle that they thought he was stupid, unable to perceive his deeper meaning. When he laughed in the wrong places they looked at each other in perplexity, but when you had reached Robert's level the comedy of life was revealed to you as was any pretence to seriousness. But behind his fatuous mask he regarded them both with deadly seriousness, behind his snickering expression he regarded them both with lethal severity.

'Go on, Rob, have another glass,' John, the schoolteacher, said, using Hilliary's abbreviation, which now made Robert feel sick.

Even with his new other-worldly licence he could find no proper compassion for this despicable cretin, for Hilliary's brainless paramour. He saw this as a personal failing and momentarily felt mean and inferior. John reached across with the bottle and poured, glancing up at Hilliary, as if a plan hatched between them earlier was showing excellent progress. And from their position Robert could see that it was all a devious plan, an insidious strategy, of that Robert had no doubt. His purpose there was to appear a clown, to give them something to laugh about after, when he was gone. They had seen themselves falling back in their armchairs and wailing boisterously. He knew that Hilliary detested him, regarded him as a shabby, abject has-been. A wretched burnt-out artist, who would never flout another breakthrough. He even suspected that she had literally manufactured a bogus love for this witless schoolteacher in order to leave him, Robert, and let him suffer in unmanned isolation, clutching a greased downward spiral, deriving immense satisfaction from the knowledge that she had truly ruined his life. Totally unable to imagine what he had done to her to deserve such treatment, he thought she could only be demonically possessed. He could see this now (see it in a brilliant, flawless light); how outwardly she had remained the same, deceptively unchanged, while inside a wretched sentient malignancy gripped her. She had become utterly corrupt, and this was why her fate had been decreed. The infinitely greater teacher of righteousness had decided on her compassionate annulment. Robert had felt the power building up since he had arrived and now he felt engulfed by an invisible, sacred fire, one from which he himself was protected.

'I've had enough,' Robert said, placing his hand over the glass. 'Really enough.'

In the face of Hilliary's bemused expression Robert slowly stood up from his chair, head a little bowed, hands on the table. He remained like that for several seconds and then turned and walked towards the door. Outside, at the end of the passageway his coat was pronged on an old-fashioned coat stand. In one of the pockets the gun crouched, loaded, the uninvited guest. He went over and took it out, like a man from a different generation after his pipe and tobacco tin. He looked at the gun once as though he suspected it had the sentient capability of expressing itself prior to doing what he expected it to do, saying something at profound variance to the inevitable brutal barks that would end everything. He walked back into the room with the gun by his side and saw Hilliary's and John's heads, which had practically been leaning together in surreptitious consultation, jump apart. Then they were beginning to get to their feet with shared puzzled expressions. Hilliary put out a strangely comical staying hand, but her open mouth remained inarticulate, silent. John, the schoolteacher, pointed at the now risen gun, as if, ironically, giving it permission to speak. Robert, easily adept, lifted the gun a little higher and without hesitation fired, emptied the barrel. He hadn't prepared a speech. All the words that came into his mind seemed pathetically superfluous. And he heard nothing from the gun for a while and wondered why the room was full of smoke. From where he stood he could see his wife sprawled on the floor and John, the schoolteacher, collapsed back in his chair, as if flabbergasted by a correct answer given by the class dunce. Robert stood still for a minute or two then picked up from the table a half-full glass of wine and finished it, gulping noisily, after which he quickly left by the back door. As his ordinary physical heaviness came back by degrees, so correspondingly the gun lost its weight and seemed, finally, to disappear.

CHAPTER FIFTEEN

He should have remembered to bring a plastic bag along, he thought, these small things can be so important, more so than can be imagined in advance. Now from his still-dripping towel was probably a liquid bean trail leading from outside the library straight to the chair he sat on, only his eyes were too blurred in confusion to see properly. But if a security guard picked up on this he would soon be over, demand in no uncertain terms that he left. After all, what did he think he was doing, messing up such an immaculately kept floor? This would mean extra work for the cleaners when the library was closed and no doubt they would want more pay to cover the unforeseen trouble. But there was nothing he could do about that now and should he be chided and chucked out, so be it. He had too much on his mind to worry about, really worry about, than let himself get over-concerned about trivialities, trifles. His struggle to contend with the black forces (without any perceptible success) came first. He had to prevent *all that* from overwhelming his present consciousness, contain it, keep it within manageable limits. He suspected though, that he would no longer be able to control outer boundaries, that, like the water he had recently emerged from, what he now knew wouldn't respect artificial banks. He felt safe now – as if there was always more room in so many books to sponge up pernicious memories – but soon that would wear off and profound doubt would descend again.

How quickly it had all come back to him, and yet he recalled it in chronological time. No fast forwards or backwards, with flashing images. Only realistic sequences allowed, though later he'd observed excessive sentiment could retard a scene. Then on going out for a late walk before bed the previous evening he had felt free from it all – suddenly wonderfully free, no physical or mental suffering. The water had just stopped exerting its power over him. Suddenly all had declared itself to be a great mistake, a great inexplicable mistake, that he had been suffering for nothing, no ascertainable reason, nothing more alarming than a prolonged bout of indigestion. And a headache. Episodic migraine. Hadn't his father (knowledge of his early life he now accepted as ordinary un-rescinded memory, memory going unobscured back to its roots) suffered from neuralgia, severe turns of nervous head pain? He had gone to sleep blissfully thinking that he was cured, but in the morning his remission was over (how doubly terrible are these respites) and the pain returned. A metal wrench hooked into his chest dragged him out of bed and he knew within a moment or two that he would be at the pool before the morning – the hour – was out. He knew that the pain would not go away and that his freedom from it during the night walk was over, nothing more than a freak exemption, a very temporary let-up, interval. He could wish and dream and desire all he liked during a period of remission, but he would always be back – *it* would always be back, to torture and mislead him. All rest from suffering was illusion, merely a time for the pain to regroup, intensify. Yet surrender, voluntarily yielding, was an appreciable mitigation of what racked, afflicted. He felt considerably less anguished as he rolled up his swimming trunks, the fight out of him, giving in to the aggressive bullying was certainly an unambiguous abatement he couldn't ignore.

The closer to the pool he got, the pain, the attraction, became merely forceful, a forceful attraction, with hardly any physical discomfort, but if he thought for a moment to turn back a sudden uneasiness struck him, and he knew that it was best to continue his way to the pool, not entertain any vain ideas of escape. Once finished with purposeless struggling he was able to appear quite normal, just like any other bather, and when he paid his money at the window he had received a nice smile from the woman dispensing tickets, whom before he'd had difficulty in seeing properly because of the thick glass or Perspex of the top half of her booth. He didn't know when the occasional swimmer became a regular swimmer, but obviously he had crossed that mark in her eyes. But this didn't mean that his apprehension of other bathers had increased. Unlike his perception at the library he had never thought that some bathers, swimmers, were peculiarly familiar. In fact they had always appeared strangers to him, as if the water washed all identification from their faces, purged them of previous individuality. Only the lifeguard he looked out for, and this time as usual he saw him stalking the edge of the pool, where on the surface of the water distorted reflections like large, loose, animated rubber bands created intricate, interlocking, patterns. The lifeguard gave him a nod, and a little professional smile. This struck Robert as odd, but there had always been something odd or unusual about the lifeguard. He was like a bull standing in the corner of a misty field. Once inside the cubicle Robert quickly and methodically undressed and got into his trunks. He piled his clothes neatly on the bench and his jacket on the single hook provided. He put his shoes under the bench not wanting them to get splashed by water coming in under the door. The short doors were the only thing he disliked about the cubicles. Looking over the top of the door before going out the augmented pull of the water almost choked him. He staggered back with both hands at his throat as if struggling to loosen the hands of a killer's hold. This seemed a very palpable, physical grip and he almost slipped on the wet floor. Then as quickly as the constriction had overwhelmed him it was gone and he could breathe freely again. His windpipe was unobstructed and he felt marvellously alive. But he sat on the bench for a time before going out to face the watery bedlam.

A cannonade of bellyflops from the far end of the pool (weren't there special times, days, for school parties? How had this clique got in?) disturbed him and the pain dug in again, behind his eyes and at the back of his knees, though his heart felt threatened too, pounding excessively. He looked about and the clamour seemed ready to burst his eardrums. It would be so easy to go back to the cubicle, dress, and be out of here. . . . He was relieved when the schoolkids growing bored headed, slithered disjointedly, in the direction of the refreshment room. Not having had breakfast that morning himself a pinch of hunger penetrated his sheath of pain, the rallying spasmodic cramps, and for a moment he wanted to visit the tea room, enjoy a hot cup of something and a couple of slices of toast. But before his mind could spell out the word *delicious* he realised that such innocent treats now belonged to a different world. A world he had taken for granted and now was lost to him. And what you have irretrievably lost teases your nostrils like a burnt sacrifice. But the simple distraction wasn't to last and soon the water below called to him like a choir of begging memories, a chorus from the beseeching past. He got down on his knees and prodded the surface with two fingers, like a doctor searching for breast cancer. All he had gone through till now had definitely weakened him and he wondered if he had sufficient strength left for that last length. For it had to be the last length even if the water's appalling magnetism called to him from the ends of the earth where he had gone to hide, no longer interested in the man he used to be, only in the man he was in the throes of becoming.

He stood up and got into the water clutching the rails both sides of the steps, letting himself down into the shallow end, then walking out deeper, till like a man descending a manhole, the circumference of the hole snug to his lowering body, closing perfectly over his head, little more seemingly left than a flattened, vaguely circular, entity, a lily pad, he disappeared. After an imperceptible pause legs flashed out, kicked repeatedly, and he zoomed off, arms creating a revolving diamond as the image lengthened, extended like a blade-thin expression of rapid movement, distance stretched out remorselessly. Almost at once he entered a state of unconsciousness, oblivious of the all-enveloping grip of water, of the swimming pool itself, even of a peripheral awareness of the outlying area. All that was gone, though his physical self continued in the element, instinctively avoiding other swimmers, weaving over and about a more target-struck figure, like porpoises at play, they let him have his way. He seemed more accustomed to this depth, his method undeviating and without sportive improvising, so obviously one attempting to break a record, no distinction between his own or another's. For it appeared then that to move so mechanically was the greatest freedom. Only inside his skull did the dreadful images live, the scene revived, replaying a life he could hardly believe was his own. Had he been turned around by some unaccountable current, walked back up the steps and into his cubicle, had the water dried on his skin like a garment over a rock under the sun, there would have been no hesitation, the round trip already completed in his mind.

Regaining partial consciousness before he reached the other end of the pool, Robert felt that he was traversing two worlds at once. Yet within moments he was very much at one with that of the swimming pool, as he ruptured the surface of the water and the chaos – shouts, laughter, cries, strident obscenities – crashed about his ears. Weakly, fearing some kind of damage he couldn't locate, he reached the other bar. He felt bruised and battered, twenty years older. The memory like a boat he kept at bay with a pointed stick. But each jab was like a self-impalement. He had become the tusked creature he had run in fear from. The sharpness of his own thrusting made him look in every direction and upwards he saw the lifeguard crouching down on the side, a new pair of goggles pushed up to the middle of his head, a caricature of concern in small, set-back eyes. One arm was poised on an upraised knee, while the fingers of the other hand languidly touched the surface of the water, like an array of twigs at the end of a broken branch. He had a very tired, apathetic, sinister look now, one that Robert immediately shied away from. In fact Robert had never liked the lifeguard, thinking that there was something strange or untrustworthy about him. He knew very well what the water was capable of doing to certain individuals and so thought that in ordinary life, away from the pool, the lifeguard could be a different man altogether. Robert thought that the lifeguard had failed to accustom himself to the job, or found it too undemanding for his natural gifts, his somewhat ambiguous amphibian nature. He was like a sea creature trapped inland. He seemed nevertheless to think that there was nothing much wrong with Robert, that he hadn't exhausted himself again, that he didn't need to be told, obliquely, to take it easy – or that he wasn't prepared to recognise Robert's particular brand of debility. Still, Robert smiled reluctantly and swayed over to the steps (he had never attempted to lever himself out of the pool as he'd observed others do, fearing a self-accusation of gymnastic exhibitionism).

He sat in his cubicle drying his hair without any enthusiasm, the shocking memory having left him numb, unreacting, practically dummy-like. Sometimes though he would have a desperate spasm and be on the verge of going back in for another swim (you could in theory stay there all day on the same ticket, a liberty allowed because rarely if ever taken advantage of), something unprecedented, something the lifeguard would raise an eyebrow at, possibly dig up a rusty regulation for not letting him in again. Not that he could face an undiluted memory directly after what he had just recalled, but he could stick to the surface, keep his head above water, be just another ordinary un-remembering swimmer for once, instead of going under for those minnows that once swallowed turned into sharks, whales. How Robert had envied those without the knowledge of the greater, threatening depths of yesterday, those who could lift their heads from the water without disturbing perspectives slicing through their heads, rearranging their psyches. Though already his mind was tender, painfully sore with the act of denial, cudgelled with ineffectual suppression. Really, he had no long-term defence against it. Every thought that bounced off the terrible memory only served to reinforce it, was eventually drawn into it, into its fermenting mass. Before he'd not known that he had a 'trigger finger', now as he studied his hand he observed his twitching forefinger with aversion. It was almost as if an obscure but obscene gesture was in the making. He wasn't surprised that he hadn't been caught. There's always a certain percentage of crime that goes unsolved. Murders that decay in files for decades, occasionally attracting the superior mind of a young detective, or become the obsession of an old, grizzled one.

But he did wonder as to the fate of the gun itself. What river had received it, as awakening from a trance he had dropped it over the side of a bridge, with no more disturbance as it struck the still water than a single rap on a snare drum? What backstreet dustbin un-emptied for years was it buried in?

Dressed, he felt indisputably the murderer his memory insisted he was, while when half naked he had felt too unformed or innocent to regard himself other than as the un-culpable swimmer he had seemed to others at the pool. How clothes defined the sinner, the grim, lacklustre criminal, though straight from the water he had acquired a suspicious sheen not to be entirely dismissed. He put on his shoes and knew that he was beyond redemption. He wondered what reprehensible lives other swimmers prepared themselves for as they got dressed in secret cubicles. Peering over the door he watched the lifeguard patrolling the edge of the pool, hands clasped behind his back, frowning slightly, hardly conscious of those he might suddenly be called on to rescue, and then realised how impatiently the lifeguard waited for the pool to close. When alone he allowed himself half an hour in the water, showing off his skills to no one in particular, spiralling from the boards, swimming like a gold medallist from one end to the other, rescuing with superb dexterity an imaginary punter. Now though, like some condemned, mythical hero he was forced to walk the pool's edge in futile expiation for a crime he couldn't forget. Robert put a foot up on the bench to tie his laces, grimacing as the nightmare, the recovered memory, extended its sharp, pointed spines into his brain, stifled a scream of insufferable dismay.

Briefly, on leaving the pool, standing in a weak shaft of sunlight, he felt curiously liberated. From all that had been tearing him apart he was delivered. At least he seemed no longer mad. He could see by the way it had been un-specifically wired into his memories that it had been a kind of meta-motivational impulse in his life, but that was over now. He had been repressing the knowledge all along, in both worlds and in the dark hiatus between, and from the start (even in this unresolved turnaround) when he had literally found himself alone in his room, his mind crowded out with forgetfulness. But all that was over, gone, because no matter how tragically, he had acted like a man. There was no excuse for what he had done and that in a very profound sense made it perfect. He had stepped outside the conceptual universe of good and evil and had seen all stripped of falsehood. The light that had shone (from a source outside all sources) on his forehead had nothing to do with justice, judgement, or condemnation. Forced to return from whence he'd come the inexpressible guarantee of indemnity had been lost and he had to accept what this corrupt, fallen world had in mind for him – what by direct responsibility he had in mind for himself. Only a continuing – blurred – perception of a recent time when he had known nothing of himself and his actions gave him a sense of being punished already and therefore being free to go his way untrammelled. Yet the memory (still equipped with a sense of undissolved autonomy because of its long absence, unavailability) allowed no such consideration, was its own judge, victim and executioner. The memory was the ultimate sentence he could hand down to himself.

Now that he knew all (although no one could know himself that well without terrible misgivings and he was already inventing alibis for supposedly lesser matters), the floating sense of unreality he'd had since he'd first started using the library as a daily refuge was peculiarly intensified. Other readers, sanctuary seekers, some of whom had once appeared familiar in a way he couldn't analyse, now looked unrecognisably ordinary. Whatever strange intimacy they'd once had for him no longer registered on their downturned faces. (On the way in he hadn't received his usual nod or smile from the counter staff. He hadn't been exactly ignored, but seemed to have slipped by like a ghost.) Now, struggling with the painful process of assimilating the horrendous memory, he thought that he would give himself up to the police. He would just walk into the local station and . . . and . . . Of course they would be surprised, but nowadays they were sent on all sorts of courses and would be familiar with all kinds of psychological complexities. There could even be a particular department for amnesia. Obviously losing his mind for a period had helped him regain his sanity. Or had he regained it earlier, at the scene of the double murder? His real sanity, the one wrecked by treachery. Had he closed the back door only to confront a narrow street dazzling, brilliant with exonerating sunlight?

A member of staff pushing a book trolley went by at what seemed an extraordinary speed, saw him, and gave him a silent, childlike wave. Chuffed, Robert waved back. Still, he would have to give himself up, officially. He would miss the library and it would always have a place in his heart. But his conscience decreed that he shouldn't take advantage of a dysfunctional detective system. He would turn himself in even if that meant making a citizen's arrest because he was a different man now. Going over the memory again and again (and he knew this would never end, that he would spin the wheel of memory endlessly, strengthening the images rather than abrading them) it was just too painful to keep to himself. For wasn't this the archaic notion of a conscience, that in policing one's wrongdoings it discouraged the conscious or unconscious devising of others? Had he been content to have remained without a past he could have started over with a new life, one without implacable remorse, without the terrible compunction he now endured. But that wasn't to be so. He had discovered the swimming pool, its revivifying waters where his memories were buried, hard, scathing, indestructible, like files inside cakes. As when all appears too awful to contemplate and yet a little light promises to break through the gloom, Robert found himself laughing (loud enough to set off a fire alarm) and a library guard came over to escort him off the premises.

CHAPTER SIXTEEN

The shouts, splashes and cries became more remote as he sat there, hidden, like noises from a radio on a beach. It was his second time at the swimming pool that day and his sense of unreality intensified by the minute, augmented by the fact that he was in a different cubicle. Swimmers got very attached to their regular cubicles, although the ticket they get at the booth contains no number (and the cubicles weren't numbered) or any indication as to the one they should occupy. But because of this attachment swimmers can usually rely on occupying 'their' cubicle. But not this time. And although practically identical Robert was very conscious, made sharply aware, of being in a cubicle not his own – and on his second time in that day. So he sat there feeling very strange, because there was something wrong with the harmony or interconnectedness of the place. He hadn't seen the lifeguard yet and so hadn't experienced that peculiar embarrassment he knew that he would for having sneaked back, for having done something out of character. The lifeguard didn't seem to derive pleasure from belittling others (from his physical superiority or swimming prowess), but Robert had felt occasionally disconcerted by what he thought were the unnecessary attentions when the trouble he was in was (he himself assessed) very minor. So he had been spared what would have been the lifeguard's quizzing stare so far.

Already on his painfully self-conscious path from the booth to the alien cubicle he had suffered what amounted to a split-second hallucination. In the blink of an eye a fleeting pattern of bathers' capped heads had made the pool look absurdly cobbled. As if the pool had been transformed into a solid space of small, half-buried, rounded stones. In the next moment this surreal vision was belied by the return of noisy movement. But while it had lasted Robert's heart had almost stopped. And he had stopped dead, frozen, a stance that had it been seen by the lifeguard would have gone bad for him. A negative construction would have been put on this abrupt immobility and Robert could almost certainly have expected additional, oblique surveillance, the kind of subtle scrutiny only the lifeguard was capable of without appearing to pry or be anxiously regarding a specific swimmer as he continued to pace the pool's edge in a cloud of boredom. Fortunately nothing else had happened to distract him as he carefully walked to the cubicle (except to find 'his' cubicle locked, which had threatened to have a *petit* incipient panic attack circling his chest) and now he sat inside, safe and sound, if feeling eerily detached from things, a little physically removed from his immediate environment.

In the end he'd had no choice but to return. Defenceless against his last memory he had decided, finally, that giving himself up to the police wasn't the answer to his problem. The memory could well wear thin in time, like the face of a coin after a few tours of mass circulation, but before that he had years of misery to see out, years of haunting, anguished recollection. If he was chased out of the police station by a dog trained to sniff out lunatics he would be slung in a cell with nothing to pass the time but to read naff library books and be subjected to constant repetitions of the scene he most wanted to escape from, the scene that probably prized itself so much that it had had copies made. (Only now were people beginning to realise how many different versions the mind contained of the same supposedly inimitable event.) But unable to forget it the nightmare memory would escape him, projecting itself over the prison wall, using every known technique, a horror film of such remarkable authentic naturalism that he would be babbling mad in a matter of weeks. Assigned a prison psychologist he would soon be doubly incarcerated in ever increasing excoriating analysis and still there would be no redemption. So giving himself up to the police was nothing but a vain piety (an honest admission belonging to another time). Ironically enough he doubted if the police would greet him with open arms; paradoxically they preferred the old, unsolved crimes on their books, stashed away in un-crackable computers. This was like putting down fertiliser. The crime undetected long enough provided invaluable growth and sustenance for those more relevant misdemeanours above.

So, desperation being the mother of contrivance, Robert had hit on another idea. Stunned by the obvious practicality of it while graphically afraid of what it actually entailed he decided to go ahead. He still felt afraid, or rather encoiled by anxiety, but what else was open to him? Although he hadn't fallen victim again to the inexplicable magnetism, experienced the spasms, contractions and general stiffness, he had felt a creeping apathy, a paralysis of will, that if left unattended, would have, he was certain, effectively petrified him. Left him like a stone carving of himself. So he could only go back into the pool, not to refresh what he had already retrieved (what an unimaginably sadistic idea!) but to put them back where they belong, to return his memory to the real unreachable depth of amnesia. Of un-plumbable forgetfulness. That had to be his next memory: the negation of all memory. He would be swallowed up by the biggest fish of all, swallowed up and systematically disgorged, by amnesia – the great, amorphous pool creature to which he had been constant food and from which he had constantly fed, on that mass of eggs hatched in identity. It was that identity he now arranged to give back to the shapeless water.

Robert sat on the bench, a little bent forward, holding in his outstretched arms his towel and trunks like a small conspirator that he smuggled in, an indispensable accomplice for what he intended to do. What he was after was already in the pool, swimming in watery, concentric circles, a strange shadowy something, waiting for him, waiting to provide the succour he desired above all else. He couldn't visualise it enough to satisfy himself enough, to give a semi-palpable reality to an intellectual idea. Its teeth remained shut against other swimmers because their pain wasn't enough to attract it; they weren't sufficiently wounded for the blood of memory to stain the surface. The screaming he heard had nothing to do with the danger he was more than willing to sacrifice himself to. No doubt there were swimmers in there with *poor* memories, or even suffering from the new, unreliable memory, but they hadn't necessarily committed a vile act. Like the afternoon put aside for kids, for modest school parties, there was probably a similar time for OAPs, when special chemicals were poured in to deal with putrefying flesh, festering limbs. But old people weren't interested in retrieving perfectly recalled memories, they liked what they had already, what they had done with recollection over the years. This wasn't memory, this was art. It conformed to an idealism that they hadn't encountered at the time. And it certainly wasn't amnesia. The profound forgetfulness they anticipated each morning and night was yet to attack them.

Getting his trunks on, Robert fell about in his cubicle like a drunk suddenly having the carpet of sobriety pulled from under him. His usual coordination seriously awry, he had great difficulty in concentrating, the prospect of impending oblivion no matter how desired on one level terrified on another, therefore one part of him rebelled deliriously, uncontrollably. Though by now he should have been accustomed to the temporary blackout. But this wasn't going to be temporary, the lights were going to be out for much longer this time. A blackout total and dreadful as death itself and with the resultant disintegration of the ego. Icily, he pulled at his trunks but couldn't get them above his knees, the beginning of his thighs, as if he had mysteriously thickened out; that, or the material of his trunks had shrunk, and he barged boozily against the door, almost breaking the lock, almost . . . revealing himself to the outside pool. Averagely proportioned, he still had a fear of showing himself to unfamiliar eyes. Then on the point of despair he finally wrenched them up, tightly about his waist, and steadied himself, clear-headed again. He knew there were some who liked a drink or two before going in, to improve their watery agility, something darkly frowned on by the lifeguard, who would order them out if suspicious, fully aware of the dangers of aquatic inebriation. So Robert wanted to appear nothing if not completely sober, even as he prepared to take the greatest plunge of his life.

Looking over the top of the door he realised that it wasn't too late to turn back. There was never anything final, unalterable, about getting undressed. In their usual neat pile his clothes waited to be put back on, without the expected interlude. And he needn't feel defeated. Perhaps his mind greatly exaggerated the torment and grief attached to his latest memory. Really, wasn't he merely responding to the newness of it? Had it been there all along much of the prickliness would have vanished, would surely have settled down into that category of regrettable youthful mistakes, practically understandable, sympathetically assessed, errors? But his heart told him this couldn't be the case. He knew what he had to do and no specious logic could change that. Yet there was so much row out there. Did the lifeguard's absence encourage high jinks on the boards and a sort of anarchistic boisterousness in the deep end? Robert could see several towels floating on top of the pool. He took a deep breath, inflated his chest, and opened the door. Once outside the cubicle Robert stepped cautiously along to the corner stairs, the lower half seemingly transformed into marble because of the greenish translucent light, and slowly descended. Prior to ducking his head he paused – it occurred to him – to bid farewell to his previous, incurable self.

Not while retaining consciousness had he yet completed a full length of the pool. There had always been what other people call hiccups. Or just simply memories required unconsciousness for a nest. Now he wondered if once he had regained his amnesia that simple pleasure would be his. Though of course if that happened he would have no recollection that once swimming underwater had been an altogether different and complicated experience. He would be amazed on being told by someone better informed that once encumbered with a personal history he had been driven to a certain extremity after which there was no safety in looking back. He saw himself in his next unenlightened incarnation as a proficient swimmer, even someone who would not disgrace himself on the boards. He did not see himself as applying for the job of a lifeguard, although that indeed would be a profound irony. He had not, of course, crossed out the possibility that he would never go near a swimming pool again. He would not know why, it would just be an instinctive phobia. But he might acquire many peculiar, inexplicable hang-ups. Even washing his hands in the bathroom could be an astonishing experience. He would feel a sort of weak electrical force coming from the tap and a beakerful of water during the night would send him back to a deeper dream than the one he had just come out of, completely un-recallable the next morning, but with more than just a funny taste in his mouth. Caught out in a shower would have him running to a shop awning where only a select if absent-minded group of people sheltered.

Feeling a little sleep reshaping his thoughts the pain of the memory diminished and deceptively gave the impression that he could have handled it, after all, above water. But he was now wise enough to know this wouldn't last unless he went on, gave his soul over to the silver flowing darkness. All that he now knew about himself would gradually be eroded, except the essentials for mundane existence. As if part of an instruction on a functional appliance his name too would survive, get through. Of course there would come a moment when what was left of his consciousness would believe he was down there *after* a memory and not getting rid of one and a strange evaporation would take place instead of a blissful deposit. That would prove difficult, but he would overcome it. As recognisable memories moulded into one flecked, variegated fantasy, he would be through. With nothing on his mind he would be out of danger and it would be time to surface, regardless of how far he had left to go to the bar. If he then felt bad his body would tell him so. Recent memory like a measly loan from the bank would see him over the following weeks. Intelligently invested he could start a new life. Head above water he sucked greedily at the sweet air no longer needed by the asphyxiated memories.

* * * * *

Later, in his room, Robert poured boiling water into his coffee mug and sniffed at the aroma with appreciation. He had always been amazed (he could sense amazement travelling back a long way in his soul) that coffee was allowed on sale in shops – that coffee was readily purchasable without a special – what? Dispensation. That you did not need a prescription from your GP to get it. Because really, it was very strong, so stimulating, and, it was universally agreed, so addictive. Had it, he wondered, first only been served in backstreet coffee shops, till little by little it became socially acceptable to sip it at home, alone, or with friends. Even with consenting children. He saw addicts stacked on cots in dark holes experiencing coffee dreams, some guffawing loudly, others screaming with the horrors. He took a good gulp and an equivocal memory lit up and then quickly fizzled out. He sat on the hard chair at the end of his bed, staring at the bundled-up towel and trunks on the draining board, sipping his coffee meditatively. He could recall leaving the swimming pool, even getting dressed in the cubicle, and a few, uncompromising memories before that, but not much more. There was no sensation of water on his skin. Any hypothetical freshness derived from actual immersion was lost to him, or blandly assimilated into a myriad of other feelings and so uniquely indistinguishable. Hairs on his arms were flattened and refused to stand with the razzmatazz of the past whenever he attempted to manhandle or coerce a glint of a memory as it finned by the back of his eyes. Still, he was getting used to all that now and didn't feel perceptibly deprived, didn't feel a party had been frozen behind the blackout. On the way in he had met Luis and she had seemed pleased to see him, surprised by his friendliness, as if they were recovering from a lovers' tiff. They had arranged to go out for a meal that evening.

Having nothing to remember made him feel that he had lost something of great value, but how could that be if he had allowed whatever it was to slip so easily through his fingers? He hadn't forgotten what amnesia was and so was able to comprehend the worth of abstract knowledge, an undamaged faculty he prized. Anyone with amnesia is bound to imagine large un-recallable bank accounts, or a big stately house somewhere falling into disrepair. In fact he no longer cared if he had been an international financier or an incomparable classical musician or an alcoholic drying out from a decade or two on a park bench. Recent memory with its erratic focus he had still to properly deal with, was gluey and cobwebby with flies of expired times stuck and shrivelled on its vibrating strands, over-lorded by a devil who comes to us all. He opened up his throat and poured more coffee down. The ancient philosophers were right: live more and more in the present moment and all your worries will prove illusory. Luis, with all her wonderful, spontaneous, creative, zany imagination always lived in the present moment and always looked fresh and untroubled. Well, if not untroubled, then sagaciously aware of the fleeting nature of all things. He knew that she had something going with an exercise regime that would help those with certain problems; and, she hoped, had real business potential. But this was her. He had a very strong feeling that this was very much like Luis. He felt they went back a long way, but just how long he wasn't altogether sure.

Peculiarly attracted, Robert went over to the draining board and looked at the wet towel and swimming trunks. The feeling was timeless and poignantly nostalgic. At a certain angle a nimbus of wasted energy seemed to surround the towel. Uneasily he reached out and touched the towel and almost at once a sudden charge of unexpected power flung him across the room, like a doll from the hand of a petulant child. Gasping, he stayed on the floor for a time before getting unsteadily to his feet. Hadn't he read reports about such weird happenings somehow? Every so often nature pulled a trick out of her hat that shocked you and left you breathless. A man would be out walking on a lonely road and a storm would blow up and he would be struck by a mind-boggling voltage of lightning but get off with hardly a scratch. Too much to take was literally too much to take. But this was certainly something to tell Luis about. Though for all her way-out ideas she had about her a realist streak, a stubborn resistance to the unusual. When told she would probably laugh at him. He laughed at himself. Just the kind of reaction, he thought, that was needed. He tried to forget about what had just happened and with commendable courage approached the towel and trunks and almost without any hesitation unfurled them and then wrung them out separately in the sink. This done he put them over a line used for indoor drying, spreading sheets of newspaper below. Hadn't he in the past considered it a pity that he hadn't an ironing board and iron? Doubtlessly Luis would have one or both and later he could borrow hers. Obviously he went with his clothes to the local launderette (wherever that was, he would have to find out). Strangely enough he looked forward to sitting in there and reading a newspaper or a book and occasionally giving glances to the passing traffic, wondering how he would spend the rest of the day.

AUTHOR'S NOTE

As far as I can recall, I hadn't been thinking, creatively considering the possibility, of using a swimming pool as any kind of fictional device before I set to work on this story. I had, though, been thinking about faces that were in some way peculiarly familiar, in an ordinary library environment, at least intermittently, over a longish period.

I saw the main character, unnamed at the time, latching on to them, being remotely involved with them. Would these faces eventually transpire to belong to some kinds of convict who, with erased minds, had been transported to a parallel Earth? In fact, I was still under this partially ambiguous impression when writing the first chapter (even though it bears no relationship to a typical sci-fi scene). But all this changed with Luis appearing on the scene. She literally came out of the blue and provided the writing with a new road map. I know Robert (Where do names come from? It is never true to say that at any time a character is faceless, although perhaps they'd be best apprehended when seen through a nebulous screen, but how does he or she flag down the right name? How in seeing it coming over as an inarticulate spectre is that decision made?) had a very bad, a pathetically chronic memory, practically non-existent. But I was never sure why. Unless of course he was a convict himself (and it occurs to me now that he is holed up throughout the book; he takes naturally to restricted spaces) – a convict in the aborted sci-fi story. Yet the book really got started when I decided (it was fictitiously decreed) that now was the time to write about the murderer on my mind for quite a while. A murderer with no recollection of his crime.

This was a long-unfulfilled ambition or fancy to explore the psyche of an essentially harmless man, who had gone temporarily mad. Of course, historically, such a subject has had great appeal, and my own serio-comic way of investigating Robert's erratic psychology might not be to everyone's liking. I could see that the story would revolve partly around the questions of fictional recall, ways of exploring the various techniques of 'imparting' to the reader Robert's past life. But the story would never depart from being read as a conventional novel, for too much experimental deviation would destroy what I thought of as an original idea. The idea of Robert retrieving his past (would he recall the past randomly, patchily or chronologically?) while swimming underwater in an indoor pool. But this didn't occur to me until Luis, his girlfriend, gets him to go as part of her (extemporary) exercise regime. At first I had my doubts about the strange nature (for Robert) of the swimming pool; or I wasn't willing to follow the logic of the accelerating narrative. Every idea comes in a transparent wrapper and undoing this often feels like a lack of spontaneous courage. Initially I wanted to hold back and I stiffened my neck accordingly, but then the influence exerted by the story proved too powerful and (inevitably) I allowed myself to be pulled along. I surrendered to the racing current of the tale. Memory is only useful when it can be accessed voluntarily at any given point, and when no specific disclosure is too horrendous to bear (when no specific memory is too blissful to bear, but that's another story).

Retention complete, Robert, no longer the victim of amnesia, is forced to recognise that perhaps he learns more than is good for him, that what he thought would be his salvation threatens to become his nemesis. Now he believes that blackout is the mind's way of protecting itself against self-destructive knowledge. Therefore, his decision to visit the pool one last time is both an act of bravery and one of cowardice (self-preservation). For Robert, revelation is something he can do without. And unless he can do without it his future looks bleak. He must muffle memory and ego in the shadows of the water, in the distorting, reflecting waters of the swimming pool. While we don't actually leave Robert where we found him, for we too have changed in the wake of Robert's transformation, there is a sense, a disconcerting intuition, of an undisturbed surface. Of the bland, illusory surface of a mirror once the parade has passed by. On turning the last page there is a sense that the story will begin again from the end.

Ralph McNeill